A Venture of the Heart

Amelia Judd

Cover design by LLewellen Designs
Edited by Karen Dale Harris

Published by Mitchell Davis Press, LLC

www.ameliajudd.com

ISBN-10: 1-946517-01-1
ISBN-13: 978-1-946517-01-2

To Adam, Aidan, and Addie
You'll always be my three greatest adventures!

PROLOGUE

HIDDEN in a shadow-filled corner of the pool deck's elaborate landscaping, Paxton Bennett cursed under his breath and thunked his head against the cushioned headrest of the chaise. If he believed in fate, he'd think the universe was messing with his head. But he didn't believe in fate. He believed in karma, and for the past six years, he'd made damn sure his life was determined by his own actions. He wouldn't piss away those efforts now by acting on the unrelenting and unwelcome attraction he felt for the girl strolling his way.

Eyeing her long legs and the glimpse of pale skin in the narrow gap between her jeans and the knot of her shirt, Pax drew in a slow, deep breath and let the darkness settle more deeply around him. In the summer night's stillness, it would be easier for her to spot movement than either his black hair or sun-darkened skin. With luck, Sage Somerset would pass by unaware he sat in the shadows less than ten feet away.

Then she stopped beside the outdoor shower and smoothed her silky blond hair into a ponytail, emphasizing the enticing green eyes that he could never quite forget and the depressing fact that luck was as fictitious as fate.

He muttered another curse and swallowed hard. Damn, he hated these annual trips to his parents' estate on Lake Michigan. He spent half the time in a silent, tense battle of wills with his father and the other half avoiding Sage, his youngest sister's best friend. His gut told him to fly home tomorrow, but his mom would be crushed if he ended his visit early.

A moment later, Sage undid the snap of her jeans and wiggled her hips from side to side, slowly lowering the denim. Blood rushed and his vision focused on her alone, blurring the background to inconsequential.

How the hell did she make a modest white bathing suit look so damn sexy?

He shook his head and tried to recall the reasons he needed to ignore this problematic attraction.

First, he was in Wisconsin for only a few days, just long enough to celebrate his mother's fiftieth birthday before returning to the resort he managed in Costa Rica. Second, Sage was five years younger and straight out of college. At only twenty-two, Sage looked at him with so much damn innocent admiration it made his head hurt. Third, she was spending the summer working at his father's beloved company.

Pax had no desire to spend his days in an office running the country's largest cabinet manufacturing company and had spent the last six years getting as far away as possible from his father, Bennett

Industries, and the unrelenting expectations that came with living in Silver Bay. He didn't need to blow it now by hitting on a girl who was wrapped up in his old life tighter than the jeans she'd just wiggled her way out of.

His brain understood that fact completely. When she stepped into the well-lit area of the outdoor shower and turned on the water, however, his ability to think slipped away faster than the water rushing down the drain. Pax watched silently as she tested the water with her hand before pulling it away to undo her nearly transparent button-down shirt.

Okay, enough was enough.

"Before you take off all of your clothes, you should probably know I'm here."

"Pax?" Sage yelped. "Holy buckets, you scared me!" She clutched the top portion of her shirt closed. "I didn't see you there. You'd be awesome at hide-and-seek," she said on a laugh, quickly shutting off the water and gathering her things. "I was going to do some laps. I thought everyone had gone to bed."

"Don't let me stop you." He forced a smile. Had his father warned her off his disappointing and irresponsible son?

"No worries. I don't want to be an inconvenience."

He stood, cutting the distance between them to a few feet. "You're many things. An inconvenience isn't one of them."

Sage gulped and her eyes widened in surprise.

What the hell was he doing? He needed to leave. Now. But he'd always been drawn to her, and damn if time had only strengthened the attraction.

Hoping to distract her from the idiocy of his words, Pax drew in a breath and gestured behind her. "Why were you going to shower?"

She tilted her chin up, a hint of defiance sparking in her green eyes. "Everyone is supposed to shower before getting in a pool. It's the rule."

"A rule no one follows. Ever."

"I like rules." She shrugged. "They promote safety and efficiency while setting clear guidelines for everyone."

"Wow. You have the heart of a true adventurer." He resisted a grin as he thought about her reaction to the activities offered at his resort.

"I've never been mistaken for adventurous," she said with a sheepish grin. "Being a rule follower is much safer."

"Okay. It's settled." He sat down on a chair beside the pool steps, stretched his legs out in front of him, and laced his fingers together behind his head. "I'll stay while you swim, since the number one rule of swimming is to never do it alone."

Her mouth opened and a flash of surprise crossed her face. "Huh. I guess you have a point." She tossed him another grin. "It's nice of you to offer."

"Yeah, it's a real hardship," he mumbled as he watched her turn the shower handle and remove her shirt. Eyes closed, she stepped under the water and tipped her head to the starry sky.

Deep breaths. He needed to take deep breaths and think about anything other than all that skin.

He shut his eyes and focused on the summer night's air. The scent of cut grass and chlorine stirred up memories of his childhood. Sometimes he forgot that a long time ago, before the bickering with his father had started, he'd been happy here.

He stole a glance at Sage. Bad move. Rivulets of water streamed over the curves of her full breasts, down the contours of her stomach, and into the triangle of fabric below. He couldn't look away.

"It must be nice to live somewhere warm enough to shower outside all the time," she said, unaware she held him under a spell. "Is the tropical climate one of the reasons you moved to Costa Rica?"

"No. It's a perk," he said, forcing the words through his dry throat.

"You've been there about five years, right?"

"Six."

"It's really nice you come home each year for your mother's birthday. It means a lot to your family."

He cocked an eyebrow.

"At least," she amended, dropping her gaze, "it means a lot to your mom and sisters. They love to see you."

"I like seeing them too. And I can't believe how much Ty and Grace have grown since last year." Playing with his three-year-old nephew and two-year-old niece had been the highlight of his trip so far.

"Claire's a wonderful mom. You're lucky to have such a big family."

"Are you kidding? Do you know how tough it was living with three younger sisters? Claire always nagged me to act out fairy tales with her stuffed animals, Hannah loved tea parties, and Kat used me as a punching bag." He fought back a grin. "They traumatized me."

"You loved it." She laughed, shut off the shower, and squeezed water from her ponytail. "And look how great your sisters turned out. Hannah is an amazing baker, Claire's life is firmly rooted in reality, and Kat rarely hits people anymore."

"You're right," he conceded with a chuckle. "They're great."

Sage stepped closer, a quizzical expression on her face. "Can I ask you a personal question?"

"If I say no, you're going to ask it anyway, aren't you?"

Mischief lit her eyes. "How'd you know?"

"I grew up with three sisters, remember? Fine. One question then you swim. Deal?"

"Deal," she said, sounding a little too triumphant for his peace of mind. "When you moved to Costa Rica, you left behind your family, your friends, your future at Bennett Industries. It's none of my business, but why did you give it all up?"

He'd heard the same question too many times to count since he'd dropped out of college to build a dream. If her voice had held even a trace of the anger, resentment, or disappointment his father employed, he would have ignored her. But she didn't look disappointed. Instead, her delicate brow creased with curiosity, and her wide, intelligent eyes shown with something that looked a hell of a lot like respect.

"I didn't lose my future in Costa Rica. I found it there." He held her gaze and hoped she could understand, or at least accept, the only explanation he'd give her.

She stared at him for a long moment before she sighed. "I'm impressed. I could never risk the promise of a secure future, not even to follow a dream. Lucky for me," she added with a wry smile, "the world needs boring people too."

Oh yeah, he was definitely in trouble. He needed to be careful not to fall any harder for this girl who loved his family, his hometown, and his father's business—everything he actively avoided in life.

Pax looked away. "I answered your question, now it's time to get started with your laps."

"Fine. A deal's a deal," she said, sliding into the still depths of the pool.

As she cut through the water, his pulse aligned with the hypnotic rhythm of her body, and his desire rocketed up a couple more levels. When she finally finished her laps, he jumped up to leave before he did something stupid.

"Thanks for lifeguarding." Sage climbed the pool steps, grabbed a towel, and began drying the water from her hair and face. "I'm glad you didn't have to rescue me. Giving me mouth-to-mouth on your parents' pool deck would have caused quite a scene."

His body tightened at the thought. *Shit.* If he didn't get the hell out of there, he'd be the one needing rescued.

Sage looked up to meet his eyes and sucked in a surprised breath. "You've never looked at me like that before," she whispered.

"How am I looking at you?"

Chewing her lip, she broke eye contact and stared toward the moonlit lake at the edge of the estate. Then she turned back to him, tipped her chin up, and took a shaky breath. "Like I've wanted you to look at me since the day we met."

Her expression, both hesitant and hopeful, undid him. Pax cursed under his breath again, pulled her into his arms, and claimed her lips with his.

Sage moaned and pressed against him, evaporating any hope of restraint. He tightened his grip on her warm, wet curves and deepened the kiss. He couldn't get enough—her taste, the feel of her barely covered body, her soft whimpers of pleasure.

"We need to go somewhere private. Now." He scooped her into his arms and carried her toward the lavish pool house. Thank God, it was only a few steps away.

"You read my mind." She sighed against his shoulder. "You don't know how long I've dreamed of this."

His step faltered and unease curled through him. He obviously realized she wanted him. But "dreamed of" sounded a hell of a lot more serious. He didn't want to be anyone's dream.

Pax looked into her eyes, filled with gut-wrenching infatuation, and the enormity of the mistake they were about to make slammed into him.

He dropped her feet to the ground, took a step back, and jerked a hand through his hair. "I'm sorry. I don't want this."

"I don't understand." She gestured vaguely toward the lower half of his body with a flustered expression.

"I do want you." He blew out a breath. "Physically."

"Ah. Just not the rest of me." She wrapped her arms around herself and looked away. "Got it."

"Damn it, Sage. I'm not trying to hurt you."

"I know." She turned back to meet his gaze, tears gathering in her eyes. "But I still think you should go."

Hands fisted, he stood motionless, despising the mixture of frustration and helplessness flooding him. Tired of disappointing every damn person he knew in Silver Bay, he strode from the pool, moving Sage Somerset to the top of the long list of reasons why he planned to stay the hell away.

ONE

SIX YEARS LATER

ARMORED in a tailored blue suit and a tight chignon, Sage walked down Pembrock Bank's sterile office corridor. As the bank's youngest corporate loan officer, she had to work harder than her counterparts to present the professional image William Pembrock, demanded from his employees.

Image isn't everything, the bank's owner was known for saying in his gruff voice. *It's the only thing.*

Sage drew in a deep breath and toyed with her classic string of pearls. She wondered why the owner's son, William Pembrock II, had summoned her to the unexpected meeting. There were no loan requests currently assigned to her big enough to draw Will's attention, and he was far too professional to call her into his office to talk about their personal relationship.

Not that there was much to talk about. They'd started dating a little over a month ago and had gone out on a total of four dates. An inch taller and a few years older than her, Will had light brown hair and nice features. While her heart didn't race at the thought of him, they were a good fit, and Sage believed compatibility beat a quickened pulse any day of the week.

She stepped inside his large corner office on the top floor and stopped short when she saw Ann Bennett, her best friend's mother, sitting in one of the leather chairs stationed in front of Will's polished black desk.

"Please join us, Sage. Mrs. Bennett and I were just talking about you."

Ann rose from her chair with a warm smile. "It's so nice to see you, dear. It's been over a week since you've stopped by the house. We've missed you."

Sage smiled as the older woman pulled her in for a quick hug. "I've missed seeing you, too. This nasty January weather has sent me straight home to hibernate most evenings."

"I'm relieved to hear you find the weather frigid," Ann said. "Because I have a favor to ask of you, and I'm happy to say it would involve much warmer temperatures. Please, let's all sit down, and I'll explain why I'm here."

Sage felt a rush of affection for the impeccably dressed, impossibly kind lady. Ann's daughter had been Sage's college roommate. Kat had taken Sage under her vivacious metaphorical wing and insisted she spend countless weekends, school holidays, and even summer breaks with her in Silver Bay. Kat's parents loved how Sage's responsible personality balanced out Kat's more unpredictable tendencies, and Sage loved everything about their traditional family. Ann had stayed home to raise the children, and Kat's father, Richard, owned the country's largest cabinetry company.

While the Bennetts occasionally bickered, they clearly loved each other. More importantly, neither parent ever walked out on the other one. The complete opposite of Sage's mother who changed boyfriends more frequently than Ann Bennett changed handbags.

"As you both know," Ann began, directing her attention to Will, "my son, Paxton, has applied for a substantial loan from your bank to purchase the resort he works at in Costa Rica."

Sage tensed at the mention of Pax. At least she no longer ached when she thought about him. Thankfully, his name now only made her cringe or curse, depending on her mood.

"I've heard there's some concern about the amount of the down payment." Ann paused. "I'm also aware you're sending Rita Wetherbee to evaluate the resort in person next week."

Will blinked. "You have excellent sources."

"I think of them as friends who care enough to pass along information regarding my family."

"Yes, of course," he said quickly, dipping his head in concession. "I didn't mean to imply otherwise. How can I help you regarding this loan request? Are you asking me to guarantee its approval?"

Bennett Industries was far and away Pembrock Bank's largest client. Will would give his precious Porsche to the cleaning lady before he'd risk upsetting Richard Bennett's wife.

"Oh, no. Nothing like that," Ann said. "We don't expect you to approve Paxton's loan as a favor to us." She smiled across the desk at him. "I would simply like the bank to send Sage to evaluate the resort instead of Ms. Wetherbee. Sage is excellent at her job, and whatever decision she makes regarding the loan will be the right one."

Sage sucked in a breath and scrambled for a reason to refuse. She didn't want to see Pax across a busy coffee shop, let alone spend a week at a tropical resort with him.

"I'd love to help," she lied, "but I'm swamped with work here." Plus, there were snakes in Costa Rica. A lot of snakes. And Pax.

Ann turned to her, disappointment and worry etched on her delicate features. "I'm sorry, dear. I didn't realize how much a week away would be putting you out." She sighed heavily. "I understand if you're unable to help me."

"I'm sure Rita will do a topnotch job," Sage said weakly.

"Nonsense," Will interjected. "I'll transfer Sage's workload to Rita. If you would like Sage to go, consider it done."

"Oh, how wonderful." Ann clasped her hands together and rose from her chair. "Thank you. It's so nice to have friends you can count on." She turned to Sage. "Will you be a dear and walk me to my car? I don't like navigating the winter sidewalks on my own anymore." Ann slipped her arm through Sage's and led her from Will's office.

Sage walked with her in silence until they reached the lobby. "You jog outside four times a week in the winter. And you're one of the best skiers I've ever seen. I'm surprised to hear sidewalks with more salt than fast-food French fries suddenly concern you."

"I sometimes forget how well you know me," Ann said with a bemused smile.

"So why do you really want me to go to Costa Rica?"

Ann pulled her to a stop near the bank's front doors. After glancing around to make sure their conversation wouldn't be overheard, she took both of Sage's hands in her own and squeezed them.

"I need to know if my son is happy."

"What?"

"If Paxton left Silver Bay simply to avoid his father—to hide from Richard's expectations—then it's time for him to come home."

"I'm not sure—"

"But," Ann interrupted gently, "if he is truly happy in Costa Rica, if he has built a good business and a good life there, then I'll be happy for him no matter how much I'd rather he was here with us."

"Wouldn't it be better if you spent the week there instead of me? Or maybe Kat? You both know him much better than I do."

"I promised Paxton I would never visit him in Costa Rica without an invitation." Frustration edged Ann's voice. "I've dropped many hints, yet my stubborn son has never asked us to visit. And Kat hasn't been herself since moving home from DC. She's even more unpredictable than usual," she said on a sigh. "I need you to spend the week with him. Evaluate his business for your bank like you are being sent to do. When you return home, I'd simply like to hear what his life there is like."

Sage stepped back, shaking her head. "I can't do that."

"I don't expect you to act like a spy or dig for details. I'd just like someone I trust, someone I love, to check on him for me." Ann squeezed Sage's hands again. "Please. I need to know he's happy."

Jeez-o-Pete. Sage blew out a sigh of resignation. What kind of person would she be if she refused to help after everything Ann had done for her over the years? "I'll do what I can."

"That's all I ask." Ann released Sage's hands then began looping a red scarf around her neck. "How are things with Will? Is it going to be hard to leave him for the week?"

"No." Sage laughed. "We aren't stupidly, madly in love. We're both approaching this relationship as adults. In fact, Will likes to say that we make a smart couple."

Ann raised a well-groomed eyebrow. "Just be careful. Unlike ventures in business, ventures of the heart are rarely logical and never clear-cut."

"I think a fortune cookie told me the same thing last week," Sage teased with a wink.

Laughing, Ann pulled Sage in for another hug. "Safe travels, dear."

Sage watched the older woman cross the parking lot and climb into her streamlined luxury SUV. Ann might not value logic when it came to matters of the heart, but Sage intended to make well-thought-out, safe, and, yes, logical decisions in all areas of her life. Spending time with the only man ever capable of pushing her past the point of logic would be challenging but not impossible.

She could keep her cool around Pax for one week. If she wanted her future to continue down the right path—the smart path—she didn't have a choice.

TWO

PAX paced the confines of his office for the hundredth time in the last hour. He needed to be tiling the bathroom of the new villa or replacing the warped floorboard on the deck of the popular oceanfront unit. Hell, he'd rather be doing office work than waiting for Logan to return from the Daniel Oduber Airport with Ms. Wetherbee. Entertaining a loan officer wasn't his idea of a good time.

It still pissed him off he had to ask Pembrock for the loan. He tried to limit ties to his hometown. Unfortunately, the first five banks had rejected his request, saying he didn't have enough cash to put down on the deal. Unless he could come up with a large down payment, the banks felt he wasn't invested enough personally in the success of the resort.

That still burned. For the past twelve years, he'd devoted his life to La Vida de Ensueño. He considered the Guanacaste region and the small, environmentally friendly and socially responsible luxury resort as his home. From hiring staff, to linen selections, to the construction of the property's new villas, he'd either made or approved every major decision at the resort since the beginning. That sure as hell felt invested to him.

At first, both Pax and the resort's owner, Charlie Applegate, had been enthusiastic about La Vida's bright future. Over time, however, Charlie had moved back to California, and his interest in the resort had waned. Less than a month ago, he'd informed Pax a large hotel chain had made an offer to purchase the resort. The chain's management was opening a new line of boutique hotels, and they thought La Vida—minus its unique social outreach program—would be a great fit.

No way would Pax let his resort turn into a lifeless clone without a fight. He planned to match the offer and buy La Vida himself. Unfortunately, every damn bank kept saying no.

His last name was the only reason Pembrock had agreed to even consider his loan. After spending half his life trying to be more than Richard Bennett's son, Pax had used that status to force the bank's hand. A knot tightened in his chest. Maybe that made him a fraud—maybe he wasn't anything more than a rich man's kid. But he would play whatever card he had if it saved La Vida.

He cursed again and shoved a hand through his hair. Logan should be back by now. He'd texted Pax over an hour earlier from the airport that the loan officer was smoking-hot and even offered to seduce her for the cause if necessary. Pax knew his friend meant it as a joke, but he needed this loan so badly he might take him up on the offer if it were serious. Logan's Casanova tendencies had caused enough problems in his role as one of the resort's adventure-tour guides. It might be time to put his talent of charming the ladies to good use.

Finally, Pax heard the low hum of the Land Rover's engine and the crunch of gravel beneath its wheels as it pulled to a stop in front of the hacienda. He charged from his office, through the lobby, and strode out the arched double-door entry, ready to greet the loan officer with his friendliest smile.

Logan hopped from the driver's seat and hustled around the front of the SUV to the other side. He shot Pax a grin that usually meant trouble and opened the passenger door. As the loan officer reached back inside to gather her things, Pax got a view of a great ass wrapped snugly in a light-gray skirt and long, trim legs balanced on a pair of shiny black heels.

His mood started to lift, the week ahead suddenly seeming more enjoyable than he'd anticipated. Then the loan officer turned from the car and locked her cool green eyes on him, knocking the smile from his face and the air from his lungs.

"Hello, Pax. It's good to see you again," Sage Somerset said in an icy tone.

And with those frigid words, karma kicked his ass and blew his dreams into a million tiny fragments.

•••

Sage might have actually enjoyed the horrified silence if she weren't so stressed out about seeing Pax again.

His mouth hung gratifyingly open for a full five seconds. Then he ran a hand through his black hair, and memories of those hands pulling her firmly against his body washed through her. She'd never wanted anyone the way she'd wanted him. Which was probably why his rejection had hurt so damn much.

He was bigger than she remembered, not taller, just more muscular. His shoulders were so wide they stretched the limits of the charcoal cotton shirt that fit him snuggly enough to reveal his sculpted arms and chest but hung loosely over the waist of his well-worn jeans.

His hairstyle hadn't changed. Straight and silky, his hair was still long enough for him to run his fingers through—his favorite gesture of annoyance—but too short for a ponytail. He hadn't shaved this morning. She'd expected him to be clean-shaven and dressed in business clothes. She should have known Pax would do things his way. Dressing to impress a loan officer wasn't in his DNA.

Logan, the man who'd driven her from the airport, cleared his throat. His gaze darted between them. "You two know each other?"

She looked at Pax and raised her eyebrows in silent inquiry.

Pax took a deep breath. "Sage is a friend of my youngest sister. She's spent a lot of time at my parents' house in Wisconsin over the years." He paused. "Our paths have crossed a few times."

She narrowed her eyes but didn't respond. His explanation wasn't wrong, only heavily edited.

"Alright." Logan made no attempt to hide the amusement in his voice. "I'll take Ms. Somerset's bags to her villa."

"Please, call me Sage." She smiled at him, purposely turning her back to Pax. "Honestly, with your accent, you could call me anything and I wouldn't mind. Where are you from, Australia or New Zealand?"

Pax grunted behind her. Good. He should know she found plenty of other men attractive.

"Australia. Beautiful country, but leaving was the best thing I ever did for my love life. American women are very receptive to my accent." He opened the back of the SUV and lifted her bags out. "Let me know if there's anything you need during your stay, *Sage.*" With a quick wink and a devilish grin, he carried her bags effortlessly into the lobby and out of sight.

Sage smiled. She didn't get the vibe he meant anything by his flirting. Contrary to Pax, Logan seemed relaxed and easygoing.

"I'll give you the tour." Directly behind her, Pax's smooth, deep voice sent sparks of electricity shooting through her.

Ugh. From the day she'd met him, he'd had that effect on her. Even the embarrassment of his rejection hadn't killed her unwanted response to him.

Schooling her features, she turned to face him. "Oh, Pax. I forgot you were there."

"It's good to see you, Sage."

She smiled coolly at him. "Lying to your loan officer isn't a great way to start this evaluation. Can we just get this over with?"

A pained expression crossed his face. "Okay." He gestured with his left hand toward the resort's entrance. "I hope you'll be impressed by what you find here."

Sage took in the man Pax had become. He'd always been gorgeous, and six years had only improved his looks, chiseling his features and deepening the intensity in his golden brown eyes. If his appeal began with rock-hard abs and ended with shampoo-commercial worthy hair, there would be no problem. Unfortunately, his passion for making the world a little better place and his complete lack of self-importance were the real kryptonite to her defenses.

But no way would she let Paxton Bennett get to her this week. Never again would she allow a man to push her past the point of logic, no matter how attractive she found him.

"Let's do it," Sage said crisply as she strode past him toward the entrance to the resort. "But you should know, I'm not as easy to impress as I used to be."

THREE

SAGE walked through the arched doorway and nearly oohed at the sight. Okay, she was impressed. Not that she would tell Pax or anything crazy like that, but, holy buckets, this place embodied tropical perfection.

"Welcome to La Vida de Ensueño, or La Vida for short," Pax said.

"What does the name mean?"

"The dream life. La Vida simply means life."

She remembered Ann's request. "Have your dreams come true here?"

"Enough of them," he responded. "It's best if not all dreams come true."

She snorted, then quickly tried to turn it into a cough. She knew full well that many dreams—and in her case, every dream that had starred the man standing in front of her—were desires that didn't play well with reality.

"Let me show you the hacienda," Pax said.

Sage was happy to focus on her job. After all, Ann had only asked her to report back about Pax's life, not question him.

Pax explained that the open-air, high-ceilinged lobby served as a gathering place and the center of the resort's activity. The large room held a deep-seated couch, multiple smaller cushioned seating arrangements, and a number of scattered café tables with wrought-iron chairs.

To her immediate right sat an elegant desk and a small reception area for arriving guests. Farther into the room, a bar made of dark wood displayed a variety of fresh juices in iced carafes. In the evening, Sage imagined guests would gather around the elegant bar to enjoy a cocktail and share stories from their day.

While the room itself was lovely and very inviting, the feature that struck her most was the complete lack of an outside wall on the opposite side of the double-door entry. With only a few pillars supporting the roof, the entire room looked over an elegant infinity pool and then down the gentle slopes of the hillside to the Pacific Ocean below.

Pax mentioned the hand-carved bar and the infinity pool as two of the guests' favorite features, then led her to the kitchen through an arched doorway off of the main room. Dark wood cabinets, light stone countertops, and expensive-looking stainless appliances filled the space. An oversized wooden table, which could easily seat twelve, sat along an open wall overlooking the pool and the ocean beyond.

"*Hola*, Susanna," Pax greeted a matronly Latino woman working at the kitchen island. "Sage, this is

Susanna. She's a gifted chef who demands complete control over the kitchen and our menu." His teasing smile countered any harshness in his words. "Susanna, this is Sage, our newest guest and an old friend of mine from the States."

The chef's head snapped up and her hands stilled on the plantain she was cutting. Sage tensed as Susanna scrutinized her, looking her up and down with a scowl. "Welcome to La Vida," she said in a reserved voice.

"Thank you. It's nice to be here."

Okay, that wasn't true, but the chef's frosty welcome had thrown her off. Susanna's short, round frame practically vibrated with a protective territorialism.

"I'm hungrier than a cowboy at a vegan restaurant," a voice boomed behind them. "Susie, what kinda grub you got for me to snack on?"

Sage turned to see a husky man in his fifties round the corner into the kitchen. He had buzz-cut brown hair, deeply tanned skin that had likely never known sunblock, and the thick neck of a former athlete.

"Sorry, ma'am. I thought all the guests were out for the afternoon. I'm Brick, La Vida's best guide."

Sage shook the meaty hand he extended to her. "Brick?"

"I didn't choose it, ma'am," he said in an unmistakable Southern accent. A smile crinkled the corners of his brown eyes. "My family started calling me that when I was still in diapers 'cause I'm built like a brick. 'Course my daddy said it was 'cause my head is thicker than a brick. Either way, the name stuck."

"Brick leads many of the adventure activities we offer," Pax said. "In fact, tomorrow morning he'll be in charge of your horseback tour."

"I'm here to work, not play. Anyway, I don't ride."

"There's nothing to worry about." Pax gave her a calming smile, addressing her like she was a skittish colt. "All of our activities are perfectly safe."

Sage crossed her arms. She was surprised he didn't offer her a carrot or a sugar cube. "I'm not worried. I just don't see why it's necessary for me to participate in any excursions. I'm not on vacation. I'm here to assess your financial viability."

"La Vida is set apart from other resorts by our unique selection of activities. Not only do we have a full range of adventure excursions, we also give guests the opportunity to take part in our social outreach program."

"Social outreach program?" Sage questioned.

"Yes, ma'am," Brick interjected, enthusiasm etched on his face. "There's nothing else like it in the region. Pax and Logan have been busier setting up that program than a cat trying to bury poop under a marble floor."

Pax grimaced. "We could've lived without that visual, Brick."

"Sorry, boss." Brick turned to Pax and lowered his voice. "I was going to say busier than a two-dollar trollop on nickel night, but ladies are present."

Sage bit back a grin at the pained expression on Pax's face. "So what does the social outreach program actually do?" she asked.

Pax shot her a relieved smile. "It allows guests to get involved with the community around them. They can spend the morning reading to local school children or working on one of the projects La Vida funds in the community. We're about to landscape the playground of an elementary school. You're helping there later in the week."

She narrowed her eyes. "I'm fine with volunteering, but I'll pass on the adventure excursions."

"You could have reviewed all of our financials in your office in Wisconsin," Pax said. "There was no need for you to travel here simply to look at our books. I'm sure you realize the importance of having more than just a theoretical understanding of a business. Until you have a hands-on experience of what La Vida can offer, how can you adequately evaluate her?"

Damn. He had her there. "Fine. I'll go along with Brick on the excursions to observe, but I am not a fan of adventure. I may or may not participate."

"That's your choice." Pax dipped his head in concession. "How about I show you to your villa? It's on the beach."

After brief good-byes to Brick and Susanna, Sage and Pax walked from the kitchen to the sunny pool deck surrounding the serene bay-shaped infinity pool.

"We're walking?" she asked.

Pax gestured toward two stone paths on either side of the pool leading down the hillside. "All the villas are within easy walking distance of the hacienda. To reach yours, all you have to do is follow me down the right path."

The right path? Sage swallowed hard. Following Pax through a tropical paradise along a romantic winding path was so *not* the right path for her.

•••

Pax tried to remain patient as Sage silently studied the villa he'd selected for her. Its location, only a few feet from the beach, made it the most sought-after and expensive guest quarters on the property.

To enhance the view, all eight villas were built a few feet off the ground, each one with a private wraparound wooden deck. The interior of the villas were all the same size and design. The main room was a luxurious living space with a sitting area and a dining table for two. The open hallway led first to the bedroom and then continued into the massive tiled bathroom. The bedroom featured a plush bed, an ocean-facing wall made mostly of a sliding glass door, and flowing white linens to appeal to the romantics of the world.

He needed her to be impressed by La Vida, or he could lose everything he'd spent the last twelve years building.

"Half of the wall is missing in my shower." Sage broke her silence the moment she stepped into the bathroom at the end of the hall. "Is this villa under construction?"

Her look of dismay worried him.

"The shower is designed that way," Pax quickly explained. "See, the wall is high enough to give complete privacy, and there's a roof overhead. We simply left three feet of open air so the natural surroundings become part of the experience. You can hear the ocean, monkeys, birds, even the wind while you shower. It's quite peaceful. Most guests love the feature."

"But there are jungle creatures here. They could get in through the opening."

"Theoretically, yes." He shrugged.

"Yes!" She whipped around to face him, her beautiful green eyes wide.

He hadn't thought it possible she could be more attractive than she'd been in college. He'd been wrong.

"Don't worry. Odds are a few geckos will be the only thing to join you in the shower."

She made a strangled sound. "Snakes with legs. Geckos are lizards, and lizards are snakes with legs."

Her ramrod posture and pale expression triggered a memory. He grinned in relief. "I forgot. You're afraid of snakes."

"I'm cautious," she huffed, "not afraid."

Pax's grin widened. He knew it would likely aggravate the situation, but he couldn't seem to stop. "Wasn't it a rat snake that sent you running into my arms? What were you, eighteen? And you'd never seen a snake."

"I was nineteen, and I'd never seen a snake *loose*. I grew up in an apartment. I'd never seen any snake in the wild, let alone one large enough to swallow me whole! Besides, I apologized for assaulting you."

"True, but you still made me carry you on my back the entire way home," he said, remembering how much he'd once loved to tease her.

She shuddered. "I couldn't stand the thought of putting my feet anywhere near the ground."

He'd been visiting his family during the first summer Sage had lived in the guest house with his sister. Kat had wheedled him into taking a walk with them after dinner through the wooded trails they used to explore as kids. When they came across a five-foot-long rat snake stretched across the trail, soaking up the last of the day's sunshine, Sage had leapt at Pax like a terrorized house cat. She'd proceeded to claw her way up his front until her arms were locked around his neck and her legs around his waist in a vice grip.

Sage had always avoided risks as adamantly as he embraced them. He would bet she never drank too much, always buckled her seatbelt, and threw deli meat away a few days before the expiration date.

He hoped her aversion to risk wouldn't prove too big of a problem in her evaluation of La Vida.

"Fair warning," Sage said, "I'm calling you the second any wildlife slithers over the wall while I'm showering."

He raised his eyebrows and let her words hang in the air. Her eyes went wide, and then her cheeks flushed.

"Well. Not the exact second it slithers in, of course." Her blush deepened as she gestured toward the towel bar. "I'll dry off first. And put on a robe. And maybe even get dressed. But then I'm going to call you." She pointed a finger at his chest. "And if that does happen, you are going to find me a shower with four intact walls."

Damn. He loved how she rambled when she got flustered. Pax didn't consider himself a grinner, but he felt another one tugging at the corners of his mouth.

"That sounds fair," he said, fighting to keep the amusement from his voice. "I thought we could have dinner together at the hacienda tonight. I'll provide you with more details on La Vida so you have a base of knowledge before heading out on your first excursion with Brick tomorrow."

"I'd prefer to have dinner delivered to my villa. I've been out of touch with the bank most of the day, and I have a lot of work to keep up with while I'm here."

So she planned to avoid him. That wasn't really a surprise, considering what happened the last time they were together.

"I'll leave you to get settled, then." He'd concede tonight, but he couldn't let her avoid him all week. He knew more about the resort than anyone, and he needed time alone with her to convince her of La Vida's worth. Like it or not, Sage would be spending a lot of time with him this week.

He stepped out of the villa and turned to close the door behind him. "And, Sage..." He paused, waiting for her to meet his gaze. "If you're willing to give La Vida a fair chance, despite any awkwardness between us, I really am glad you're the one to decide her future."

"Awkwardness?" She smiled coolly. "We kissed. Only once, if I remember correctly, and that was years ago. Not a big deal."

Pax studied her a moment longer than comfortably allowed in polite conversation. The way he remembered the night, they'd been seconds from ripping each other's clothes off. She'd damn near pushed him over the edge with wanting her.

Maybe she remembered things differently. The possibility should relieve him. Instead, for some inexplicable reason, he found it depressing.

"I'll see you in the morning. Breakfast is in the lobby anytime after seven."

She held his gaze for a moment, nodded briskly, then moved to gather her luggage, dismissing him with her demeanor rather than her words.

He left her villa and started up the small side trail to his private home. No matter what lingering attraction he felt for her, he had to keep all interaction with her this week platonic. He couldn't afford to allow emotions to complicate, or even compromise, his loan request. He could ignore Sage's pull for one damn week if it meant saving La Vida.

He didn't have a choice.

FOUR

SAGE woke the next morning to a room full of bright sunshine, fragrant ocean breezes, and the active chatter of the tropical birds and monkeys outside. She stretched her arms over her head, enjoying the silky slide of her skin along the luxurious sheets, and yawned. Blatantly postponing an eventual trip to her jungle bathroom, she thought about the week ahead of her.

Any hope that her attraction to Pax had faded seemed laughable after her reaction to him yesterday. That ridiculous, never-ceasing awareness of him still sent her body on high alert when he was close. Even more annoying, her thoughts kept circling back to him even when he wasn't around. The harder she tried not to think about him, the more impossible not thinking about him became.

If she was going to make it through this week without making a fool of herself again, she would have to learn to control, or at least hide, her reaction to him. Considering that had proved impossible in the past, she should probably just avoid him as much as possible.

Thankfully, she didn't need to be near him in order to evaluate the validity of his loan request. She could study the resort's financial information, tour the facility, and even go on the excursions without him.

To fulfill his mother's request, though, she'd have to spend some time with him. Even then, how was she supposed to tell if he was happy with his life? How did you know if anyone was truly happy in life?

For Pete's sake, she didn't even know if she was happy with her own life.

Okay, she wasn't unhappy, or anything like that. Everything was fine with her life. Her job, her apartment, her future, even her dating life—all fine. So why did being around Pax already seem to make her want more?

No. Scratch that. She needed to push him from her mind, do what she'd been sent here to do, and go home unscathed. After all, crushing on a guy, offering herself to that guy, and then getting rejected by him had been a painful mistake. Doing it twice would be an idiotic one.

Unable to avoid her bathroom any longer, she climbed from bed and focused on a more immediate worry. Who knew what creatures might have ventured into her shower in the middle of the night? To make matters worse, the glass door between her wildlife shower and the rest of her bathroom had a three-inch gap above and below it. Anything could slither through.

Her overactive mind pictured her bathroom overrun with snakes and lizards of varying sizes and sneakiness. There could be one waiting silently inside her bathroom door, ready to attack as soon as she opened it.

Sage tiptoed closer. For some reason, it seemed imperative she make a stealthy approach. She slid away the bath towel she'd ingeniously rolled up and shoved beneath the door the night before. At least no slithering visitors were getting into her bedroom.

"Here goes." She took a deep breath, turned the doorknob silently, pushed the door open, and scanned the room for any reptilian invaders.

Empty.

Sage huffed out a relieved breath and slumped against the wall. If this didn't get easier, she'd have to reduce her need for the bathroom by lowering her liquid intake to a dangerous level. She'd need to check the Internet on the dangers of dehydration, which right now seemed preferable to a venomous snake.

She darted into her bathroom and showered as quickly as possible—no sense pushing her luck.

In less than five minutes, she stood in front of her suitcase, considering her options. Desperate to prepare for any situation she might face this week, she had splurged on a shopping trip two days earlier. She'd spent a fortune on new clothes from a retailer that specialized in active wear for the adventurous sort. Its ads showed men and woman surfing monster waves, climbing impossible mountains, and hiking virgin jungle trails. All the while looking fabulous, of course.

In addition to the outfits purchased for adventures she had no intention of participating in, she'd bought new business wear and sundresses—all with coordinating accessories. Her bank account had taken a massive hit. She would consider it worth every penny, however, if the new clothes helped her get through the challenging week with Pax.

For today's horseback-riding and hot-springs adventure, she chose a sporty-style bikini under slim-fitting, stretchy black pants and an equally stretchy cap-sleeved blue top with a quarter-zip. The top provided protection from the sun, and the saleswoman had assured her the entire outfit would work for hiking, climbing, or a day at the beach.

On the walk up the path to the hacienda, Sage braced herself for seeing Pax again. Even though she hadn't spent much time with him yesterday, she'd seen no unappealing changes in him.

How freaking unfair was that?

She finished climbing the winding path and scanned the area—no Pax. Her nerves eased. If her luck held, she could head out with Brick for the day and not see Pax again until dinnertime.

At the open-aired eating area of the hacienda, three tables were filled with couples enjoying a meal before heading out on their own adventures for the day. All of the couples, who appeared to be anywhere in age from thirty to sixty-something, looked like the type to enjoy a fit, healthy lifestyle. It made sense that La Vida would appeal to active travelers. People interested in a lazy vacation likely wouldn't choose to spend a week that featured adventures or volunteering in the local community.

Sage chose a light breakfast of fresh fruit, yogurt, and Costa Rican coffee from the buffet and moved to a table situated halfway between the hacienda and the pool. She closed her eyes to fully soak in the lovely morning sunshine. The gentle air caressing her skin reminded her of summer days at the Bennetts' lakeside estate.

Unlike Pax, Sage had always been happy to spend time with his parents and three younger sisters in Silver Bay. Of course, Richard Bennett had never tried to control her life the way he had tried to dictate his son's. Richard treated her like a beloved daughter whose well-thought-out decisions always made him proud.

Kat often joked that her father seemed to like Sage better than a few of his own children which was far from true. Sage knew Richard loved his kids, but he set high standards for them and could be disapproving when those standards weren't met. Unfortunately, this characteristic had hurt his relationship with each of his kids at one point or another.

"Hey, little lady. Are you ready for some riding today?" Brick's cheerful Southern drawl boomed through the breakfast area and broke into her thoughts. Although he was old enough to be her father, his smile was boy-like and so infectious it soothed her nerves about the ride.

"I'm ready to go anytime." She smiled back at him. "Just enjoying the view while I eat."

"You ain't seen nothing yet. Go ahead and have your breakfast. I'll chase down the picnic lunch Susanna packed for us and round up Pax while you finish."

"Round up Pax?" The nerves returned. "I thought you were my guide today?"

"Course I am. I'm the best horseman at the resort, but Pax made it clear he wants to be included on each of your excursions." Brick grinned so big the laugh lines around his eyes crinkled with sincerity. "I think he's happy to finally show this place off to a friend from home. Nobody he knows up north has ever come to visit before."

Sad, but not surprising, considering what Ann had admitted about Pax never inviting his family to the resort. Sage knew about the strained relations with his father, but she'd been so busy avoiding Pax for the last six years that she hadn't realized he'd been doing some avoiding of his own. Before Sage caught her flight, Kat had even complained that the time kept growing between her brother's trips back to Wisconsin.

"Plus, the way I hear it, you're a VIP," Brick announced in a voice loud enough to regain Sage's attention.

She winced when some of the other guests in the breakfast area looked her way. She shot her new audience an uncomfortable, this-guy-is-crazy-don't-listen-to-him look.

"Pax said if we don't do a good job showing you La Vida, he won't have enough money to buy her from Charlie." Though Brick had moved closer to her table, his voice never lowered. It appeared he'd never mastered using his inside voice. "Which would be just horrible since Pax has done more for this place than LeBron did for Miami."

Her heart squeezed at Brick's earnest expression. If her bank denied the loan, odds were good everyone at La Vida would be out of a job. While it was her job to study the numbers and report on the facility, she didn't have final say in granting a loan this large. She hoped everyone here understood that if Pax didn't have enough money for a down payment, Pembrock could reject his loan request, regardless of what she had to say after her week at La Vida.

•••

Sage was surprised—and way relieved—when Pax didn't join them at the car. Something must have come up, thank God. For the next hour, she sat next to Brick, listening to him point out the sights as he drove inland through rolling flatlands, areas thick with forest, and even numerous open fields with grazing cattle. A defined mountain range filled the beautiful sunlit horizon.

"Does it rain here much?" Sage asked.

"Not from November to April. This area of Costa Rica is considered a tropical dry forest rather than a rainforest. Most folks love to visit from the States in the winter when they can count on it being warm and dry here."

"I can't argue that. This weather is a lot nicer than Wisconsin in January."

"Yes, ma'am." He grinned at her. "I've lived here over twenty years and never plan on moving anywhere again that gets colder than my favorite beer." He turned onto a long drive leading into a tree-filled valley. "This is the ranch we use for our horseback tours. It sits at the foot of an active volcano. The main house is straight ahead, but we're headed to the stables which are down the hill to the left."

Sage felt her eyebrows hit her hairline. "Volcano?"

"Yep. But she hasn't blown in a few years so we should be safe today." Brick pulled to a stop.

"A few years sounds pretty recent to me," Sage muttered. Great. Now she had to add active volcanos to her growing list of worries. What would be next? Fire? Maybe a little brimstone?

At least she didn't have to worry about spending the day with Pax.

She reluctantly followed Brick down a small slope to the horse stables, which consisted of a haphazard collection of open-air structures with beams of wood supporting weathered metal roofs. Ranch hands hustled around the grounds, tending to the numerous horses corralled in the area.

"Let's find you a horse, little lady."

Sage sighed and followed Brick to the corral, eyeing the horses with skepticism. She wondered if they had a horse to fit her riding ability or, more accurately, her lack of riding ability.

"Hercules here is a nice fella." Brick rubbed the nose of the huge brown horse in front of him with a meaty hand. "He's a real gentleman and the biggest boy at the ranch. He's quiet and calm. I think you'll like him."

Sage arched an eyebrow. Hercules seemed like some sort of genetically altered species of super-sized proportions. "He's very handsome. I assume he's part Clydesdale and part wooly mammoth?"

"No ma'am. He's an American Quarter Horse."

She fought back a smile at Brick's solemn response. Whenever she evaluated a business, she never underestimated the value of the company's human assets. The ability to look beyond numbers on a spreadsheet had made her one of the top loan officers at her bank. Brick was a gem, and by employing him, La Vida earned a shiny gold star in her book.

"I think our guest might prefer Abuelo."

Tension tightened her stance and washed the ease from her smile. Only one voice could affect her so drastically. She drew in a breath and slowly turned around. Though Pax stood a good ten yards away in the open-air stable, he dominated the space, sending a ridiculous wave of claustrophobia through her.

She cocked her head to the side. "Abuelo?"

"The graying criollo at the end. His real name is Francisco, but we've called him Abuelo for years."

Sage moved down the line of horses toward the one he gestured to. While all the horses were smaller than Hercules, Abuelo's stocky frame stood drastically shorter than the others. Gray edged his light brown mane, and the big droop in his back suggested Abuelo's youth had long since passed.

"I'll take him," Sage said, confident that short and old were the perfect combination in a horse for her.

Pax nodded at her, his expression an unsettling mix of humor and satisfaction, and turned to the group of stable hands tending the horses. "Miguel, please saddle up Herc for Brick, Abuelo for Ms. Somerset, and Dandelion for me."

Sage gave an amused snort. "Dandelion? Really? Your horse is named Dandelion?"

As the ranch workers began to prepare the horses for the ride, Pax walked to a low, long counter located near the entrance. "Don't let her name fool you," he said over his shoulder. "Dandie's a tough horse to handle. She may be a real beauty, but she's stubborn as hell. Poor Abuelo's carried a torch for her for years, but she doesn't give him the time of day."

He selected a dull black helmet with a dangling chin strap from the counter before focusing a devilish grin on her that instantly fried her brain cells. When he beckoned her with his index finger in a come-closer gesture, she mindlessly complied. He gently settled the ugly helmet on her head.

"Safety first," he said as he reached to fasten the strap under her chin. When his hands brushed along her jawline, her senses ignited and certain key body parts perked up in awareness.

So much for keeping her cool.

She summoned enough composure to swat at his hands and step away. "I can handle my own helmet." Ignoring the amused light in his eyes, she fumbled with the strap. "Why did you pick Dandelion if she's such a difficult horse?"

"I've never been smart enough to take the easy route."

"Is that a strength or a weakness?"

"Depends on who you ask," Pax said.

"I'm asking you."

He shrugged. "Both."

"I'm not following you."

"Any strength carried to an extreme will eventually become a weakness. The trick is in finding the right balance."

Sage studied him for a beat. "Deep. I'm impressed."

"Impressed enough to grant the loan?" Pax's eyes lit with mischief.

"Sorry. No." She laughed, enjoying his exaggerated expression of hopefulness.

"Worth a shot," Pax said with a wink. "I'm going to help Brick load the gear. We should be ready to leave in a few."

As he walked past, every nerve ending tingled and her body tightened. She sucked in a breath. Jeez-o-Pete. Pax had been at least two feet away, and her body responded like he'd suggested they skip the ride and spend the afternoon making out instead.

Sage fiddled with her helmet and cleared her throat, her gaze darting around the stables. After all these years, he still made her fidget.

Pax Bennett was like a bad rash. She'd been forced to ignore him for what felt like forever before all the annoying symptoms of his touch faded, and then, at the slightest provocation, everything flared back up again.

"Time to saddle up," Brick yelled from beside his horse with an encouraging smile.

Chin up, shoulders back, deep breath through the nose. She could do this. At least the stress of seeing Pax again coupled with the fear of a snake attack or possible volcano eruption had put her worries about participating in risk-filled adventures into perspective. Compared to snakes, hot lava, and dealing with Paxton Bennett for a week, riding a horse seemed about as dangerous as a day at a banking convention.

While her experience with horses was limited, she did know the proper technique to mount. She prayed combining this knowledge with Abuelo's low stature would save her the embarrassment of not being able to get on the darn horse.

Sage picked up the reins, grabbed the pommel, and put her left foot into the stirrup. Abuelo snorted and glanced back to see what newbie he'd been stuck with today. Seemingly unimpressed, he shifted his weight and swatted his tail in what felt suspiciously like a dismissal.

"I'm no happier about this than you are," she mumbled and swung her right leg up and over Abuelo's back, landing lightly in the saddle. "I snuck a few extra sugar cubes from breakfast. If you get me through today in one piece, consider them yours."

"You've already resorted to bribery?" Pax shook his head in mock disappointment before he mounted his horse in one smooth motion. "The adventure hasn't even started yet." He clicked his tongue twice and Dandelion started out of the stable with Abuelo close behind.

"Speak for yourself," she grumbled as Abuelo followed Dandie, completely ignoring Sage's attempts to lead him.

Her adventure had started the moment she'd stepped into Pax's world.

FIVE

PAX settled into the back of the small group, content to let Brick lead the way. The well-worn dirt trail meandered through the dry tropical forest for miles. The wide path followed a large stream and passed by numerous waterfalls before returning to the ranch. Its natural beauty delighted every guest who traveled it. Pax had banked on Sage sharing in said delight.

Not likely, judging by the waves of tension rolling off her as she fought to keep her horse beside Brick and Herc. They'd been riding for twenty minutes, and the entire time she'd prodded her horse to keep up. Her words to Abuelo ranged from encouragement, to orders, to begging him to stay abreast with Brick. It appeared Sage wanted to keep as far away as possible from Pax.

Problem for her was that stubborn old Abuelo wanted nothing to do with the large quarter horse Brick was riding. Nope. Abuelo loved Dandie and had no intention of letting a novice rider keep him from his crush.

"It would be a lot easier to relax and let Abuelo walk beside Dandelion," Pax called. "He'll make you miserable until you do."

She puffed out a defeated sigh, slumped her shoulders, and appeared to ease her white-knuckled grip on the reins.

Sensing victory, Abuelo immediately stopped walking. The horse swished his tail at the bugs, waiting patiently until Pax and Dandie caught up. Once his true love reached his side, Abuelo resumed walking, now in perfect unison with the female horse's pace.

Pax grinned and yelled ahead to Brick, "Why don't you go on with Hercules? He's bound to get bored with our slow pace. Sage and I will meet up with you for lunch."

"Good idea, boss. See you in a bit." Brick squeezed his heels into Herc's belly, prompting the horse to trot down the path and out of sight within seconds.

Pax felt Sage's eyes burn into him hotter than the late morning sun. "You knew Abuelo was uncontrollable, didn't you?"

He schooled his features into an expression of innocence. "He's not uncontrollable. He's besotted."

She snorted.

"As a bonus," he continued, ignoring her scowl, "with Brick riding ahead of us, we have a chance to talk about La Vida alone. I know you've studied her financial records. Wouldn't you like to know more about what really makes her special?"

He waited for her response, trying like hell to maintain eye contact. Which was damn hard, considering certain parts of his anatomy begged to study the hypnotic sway of her body to the horse's rhythmic pace.

"Alright. What makes her special?"

Pax drew in a deep breath. He had to stop thinking about her long, lean curves and start focusing on what he was here to do—impress her with La Vida's uniqueness.

"While many guests participate in the adventure excursions we offer, nearly all of them take part in the social outreach program," Pax said. "Last week, a couple from Iowa spent a morning in the classroom of the local elementary school reading to the kids in English. They enjoyed it so much they cancelled their surf lessons so they could go back to work with a different group of kids the next day."

"This is common?" Sage prodded, studying him with a neutral expression.

Worry churned his gut. Her bank was his last chance. He needed to get through to her. "We've built more than a luxury getaway for the wealthy," he said, fighting the edge to his voice. "We're trying to bring different cultures together."

As their horses followed a gentle curve in the path, Pax wished like hell he could read her mind. Though she said nothing, her gaze remained locked on his. A flicker of emotion played across her face, then her expression softened.

"I can tell La Vida means a lot to you. But you've requested a large amount of money, and there's a huge risk involved. Tourism to Costa Rica could decline." Her voice rose as she began ticking off reasons. "A guest could hurt himself falling off a horse and sue you, a large storm could devastate the area, a horde of venomous snakes could slither over the ill-advised bathroom wall and attack a guest in her sleep."

Pax quirked an eyebrow. "You just took your fear of snakes to the next level."

"Okay. The last one is probably not going to happen." She waved her hand in dismissal. "But you can't deny the fact that a lot could go wrong."

"I'm not going to live my life afraid of what could go wrong. Even though we take all of the necessary precautions with running a resort of this nature, you're right, we can't eliminate every possible risk."

"I'm glad you can see—"

"But," he interrupted, keeping his voice soft, "I hope to show you that some things are worth the risk."

"Good luck with that. I spent the evening of my twenty-first birthday at a review session for a micro-economics exam because I was afraid I would do poorly if I missed it. Looking back...?" She grinned and shrugged. "That might have been a little overly cautious."

He laughed. Sage looked as chagrined over her behavior as she was accepting of it.

"You look younger when you laugh," she said, and her pretty green eyes widened in surprise. "Not that you look old," she continued in a rush. "Well, older than you did, yes, but in a good way." She rolled her lips inward, bit them shut, and developed a sudden interest in the path they were traveling.

He laughed again. He'd always liked that she rambled when she got nervous.

It felt real.

"They're much more colorful than the gulls near my apartment back home." Sage's soft voice broke into his thoughts.

He followed her gaze upward and spotted a flock of green parrots in the thick canopy of heavy limbs over the trail. "They're called white-fronted parrots. One of many species of birds in Guanacaste."

"They're beautiful."

"Glad you like them." Maybe pressuring her into taking part in the resort's excursions wouldn't backfire and cost him his loan after all.

As they continued down the trail, the nearby stream grew in width and strength, and the sound of trickling water morphed into the rush of a much stronger stream. Pax pulled Dandie to a stop when the trail split and the water curved to their left.

"We need to take this switchback," he explained, motioning to an s-shaped route down a slope to the right. "It's a gradual decline. Perfectly safe."

Sage arched an eyebrow. "You sure? It looks steep to me."

"It's fine. The horses have walked this trail hundreds of times."

He nudged Dandie forward at a slow pace, knowing Abuelo would follow. When they finished their descent a few minutes later, Sage released an audible sigh.

"Phew. I'm glad to be back on flat ground," she said, raising her voice to be heard over the sound of falling water.

"Some things are worth the risk," he said, repeating his earlier words as they rounded a sharp corner.

"It's gorgeous," she said, awe in her voice. "I've never seen water so blue."

Directly in front of them, a waterfall burst through the green foliage forty meters above, cascaded down the rocky face of the canyon wall, and landed in a celestial blue lagoon.

"It's one of nature's greatest works of art," Pax said. "Dissolved copper minerals from the volcano create the unique color. Once you swim in this water, you'll never want to go in Lake Michigan again."

"I'd like to, but I'm not sure I can." She chewed on her lip, looking skeptically at the lagoon.

He fought a grin. "There are no snakes in there."

"Are you sure?"

"Absolutely." Pax swung off of Dandie's back and gathered the reins from Sage. "I'll secure the horses in a shady area. You get ready to swim in the prettiest water you'll ever see."

After caring for the horses, Pax returned to find Sage standing next to the lagoon's edge. Facing the waterfall, her back to him, she plucked the ugly helmet from her head and shook out her long blond hair. He gritted his teeth and reminded himself to ignore the attraction.

When she slipped out of her shirt and pants, revealing a black bikini beneath, he cursed at his own damn stupidity. He should have realized watching her swim today would bring back memories of that last night in Silver Bay. His body tightened, the mist floating through the air doing little to cool him. Evidently, six years hadn't been a long enough time to wash away his desire.

•••

Sage turned to see Pax standing a few feet behind her. She scanned him up and down. Unlike her, he was still fully clothed in faded jeans and a light blue T-shirt. Which, annoyingly, made her bikini feel even more revealing.

"Aren't you joining me?"

"Nah. I'll be the lifeguard."

Because that worked so well last time? She did a mental eye roll and turned back to the lagoon, scanning its blue depths. "I can't see any snakes in the water."

"That's because there aren't any."

"Just making sure." She waded in waist deep and sighed in pleasure. She dipped her head under, enjoying the instant relief from the tropical heat. Surfacing, she slicked her hair back. "This feels amazing. Are you sure you don't want to come in?"

"I'm sure," he answered in a gravelly voice, shoving a hand through his hair.

He made her nervous pacing around the edge of the lagoon. She'd thought they'd been getting along okay, but now he seemed distracted, tense. Part of her was relieved he hadn't joined her in the water. She had a hard enough time keeping her cool when he was completely covered. She might combust if he stripped down to a bathing suit.

She turned back to the jaw-dropping waterfall, wondering if it had a treasure-filled cave behind it like it would in the movies.

"Time to investigate," she murmured. She took a deep breath, cutting through the cool water with ease.

The noise, current, and mist grew stronger the closer she got. After a few attempts at swimming directly at the base, she realized the powerful cascade made reaching it more difficult than she had expected.

She might be cautious, but she wasn't a quitter. Sage redoubled her efforts and fought through the current, swimming toward the side of the cascade rather than directly at it. She'd always been a strong swimmer and had even lifeguarded her way through college, but this challenge was testing her strength. Her breathing grew rapid and her body strained with the effort.

Finally, she broke through the strong flow. Laughing in accomplishment, she treaded water directly behind the beautiful blue curtain. She looked around to see a small cavern worn into the rocky wall about the same size and depth as the backseat of her Toyota and completely blocked from view by the falling water. Not exactly a secret cave but still a nice find.

Enjoying the peaceful setting, she gripped the rocky wall and caught her breath. After a few minutes, she let go of the edge and slipped under the water again, ready to return to the shore. Before she could push off the wall, she felt a strong arm wrap around her waist haul her above the water and backwards into a hard, male body.

Sage yelped in surprise.

"Are you okay?" Pax asked over the pounding beat of the waterfall, his voice rough with concern.

"I will be when you let me go!" She struggled against him until he dropped his arm. "What the heck was that for?" she demanded, spinning in the water to face him.

Soaking wet and fully clothed, Pax glowered at her. He gripped the rocky ledge with one hand and shoved the other through his wet hair. He looked ticked. Really ticked.

"You scared the shit out of me," he said. "I walked away for a few minutes and when I came back, you were gone."

"You walked away? Some lifeguard."

His jaw clenched. "I needed a break."

"From what? Is watching me swim that hard of a job?"

"You have no idea." He spoke so low that his words were almost lost in the sound of the cascading water.

"Fine. We can take a break now." Sage grabbed the ledge, boosted herself out of the water, and scooted over to put some extra space between them.

Pax stared at her with a hard, unreadable expression. "I thought you were hurt."

He'd been worried about her? Right or wrong, the thought was satisfying.

"I didn't mean to scare you." She shrugged. "I just wanted to see if the waterfall hid a cave full of pirate's booty."

He raised an eyebrow.

"What? It could happen," she said on a quick bubble of laughter.

"Are you a fan of pirates?"

"I admire their spirit of adventure."

"Seriously. You?" Pax asked, a smile playing around his lips.

"Don't sound so surprised. People often appreciate qualities in others they lack themselves. Take you for example. Right now, you probably admire people who remember to take their clothes off before swimming." She patted the spot next to her. "Care to join me?"

Pax sighed and lifted himself out of the lagoon. Water streamed down his face and his muscles contracted in effort. When he positioned himself next to her on the ledge, his size immediately overwhelmed the intimate space.

His sun-warmed skin smelled amazing. She drew in a long breath of him, and her gaze dropped to his mouth. His full, wet lips were parted slightly and only inches away. If she tipped her head and leaned closer, she could taste him. Her pulse kicked up, and her breathing grew heavy. She wanted his mouth on hers—had never wanted anything so much.

She licked her lips and raised her gaze to meet his. The undeniable desire burning in his eyes made her breath still. He leaned closer, and she groaned.

"Sage?" He breathed her name, a warning in the low, sexy tone.

The tone triggered a memory from the past. A memory of that night by the pool. A memory of craving Pax's touch more than air. A memory that ended in equal amounts pain and embarrassment.

Rational thought broke through the surreal scene and screamed at her to stop. No way would she let sexual desire control her.

"I have a boyfriend," she croaked.

Pax's body, no more than a second away from touching hers, stilled and his expression hardened. He gave a nearly imperceptible nod and leaned away.

Good. She felt relieved. Right?

"To be honest, boyfriend is a little inaccurate," she said, filling the silence before it became too awkward. "We've only gone out a few times, but he's got promise. He's a banker. So that's nice. I mean, he's responsible, which is nice. And other things too, of course. Like, um, punctual, logical, stable." Holy buckets, she couldn't seem to stop the ridiculous flow from spewing. "And he loves Wisconsin. We both want to put down roots there. We're a smart match," she added weakly before clamping her lips shut in a pained half-cringe, half-smile combo.

"Smart match?" he asked, his expression flat.

"I've seen what happens when boyfriends are chosen for the excitement they offer in the present. I plan for the long run instead, and Will is a good fit for my future."

"Will?"

"William Pembrock, that is. Well, the son, not the father."

"From the bank?"

"You know him?"

"Oh, yeah," Pax said with a humorless smile. "My dad loves him." He scrubbed a rough hand down his face. "Let me get this straight. You're dating the guy who has final say over my loan?"

She nodded.

"So that makes kissing you an even worse idea," Pax growled, frustration edging his words.

Before she could respond, he started for shore, swimming directly through the cascading water. Sage knew building a secure future required self-restraint, and she'd just been strong enough to stop trouble before it started. She should be giddy with pride. Or at least relieved she'd been able to resist temptation.

But did she feel either proud or relieved? No. Instead, her stupid heart squeezed with an emotion that felt suspiciously like disappointment.

SIX

IT quickly became evident Pax planned to tiptoe around her for the rest of the afternoon.

Which was fine by Sage. She didn't want to think about—much less talk about—their near kiss.

Not long after the ill-advised waterfall stop, they met up with Brick who seemed unaware of the thick tension and limited communication between her and Pax. Thankfully, Brick carried the conversation for the remainder of the excursion. By the time Sage sat with the guide in the Land Rover returning to La Vida in the late afternoon, she'd heard more than a dozen stories of his adventurous life. Not that she believed even half of what he claimed was true. Brick obviously thought embellishment and good storytelling went hand in hand.

Sage didn't care if he exaggerated. Brick's story of skiing off a mountain cliff and avoiding death by grabbing the uncovered roots of a native tree had been a welcome distraction. Like a superhero movie, it simply required a willing suspension of disbelief to enjoy Brick's tales. Plus, his easy manner and talkative personality had allowed her to keep her distance from Pax.

"And that's how I ended up exploring the Daintree Rainforest for a week with Carter O'Reilly. You know, the movie star in all those action films? Real nice guy. Kinda misunderstood though." Brick finished his latest story as he pulled the SUV to a stop in front of the resort. "Here we are, ma'am. Back at La Vida, safe and sound."

"Thanks, Brick." Sage shot him a weak smile, gathered her backpack, and bolted for the hacienda.

Pax had followed behind in his own vehicle, and he could be pulling up at any moment. She rushed into the hacienda, planning to head straight through the building for the path by the pool. She hoped to make it back to her villa before he could inform her of the next adventure he had planned for her.

Raised voices stopped her in her tracks. A peek through the arched opening to the kitchen showed Susanna pointing an accusing finger at Logan as she charged toward him.

"I lost a pastry chef because of you!" Susanna yelled. "Again!"

"Come on, darl, don't be mad." Logan backed away from the chef, both hands extended, palms out in an I-mean-you-no-harm gesture.

"Don't you *darl* me, Logan McCabe. Now who will make the croissants every morning? Who will make the desserts every evening?"

Brick joined Sage in the kitchen's doorway just as Susanna let loose with a string of Spanish delivered at a speed well beyond Sage's limited ability to comprehend. Apparently, she should have taken

57

another year of Spanish in college. Then again, judging by Susanna's tone, Sage doubted Señora Pineda would have covered the type of words the chef was currently yelling at Logan.

"She sounds really ticked," Sage whispered to Brick.

"Logan hooked up with the little lady who did all the baking. 'Cept Logan doesn't stick with any lady for long. She quit when he broke it off." Brick shrugged. "Problem is, he did the same thing a couple of months ago, so Susie is pretty steamed."

Susanna stood toe-to-toe, or rather nose-to-chest, with the Australian, her brown eyes blazing. "I swear, Logan, the next time you don't keep it in your pants, I will cut it off!" She punctuated her words with a chopping motion with her hand before storming through an opening on the other side of the kitchen.

Pax appeared in the arched doorway beside them. Sage felt the familiar sizzle of awareness even before he spoke.

"Go calm her down," he instructed.

"Okay, I'll try," Brick answered, looking unsure.

"Not you." Pax shot a look at Logan. "He's the one who seems to think his sex life is more important than his job."

"Don't worry, mate." Logan slapped Pax on the shoulder. "I'll take care of it." He winked at Sage, then headed in the same direction as Susanna.

"I better make sure she doesn't kill him," Brick said, following after them.

Pax blew out a breath. "Do I even want to know what kind of impression we're making on you?"

Sage bit back a grin. "I like them."

"They're a pain in the ass."

"Aren't all families?"

He snorted. "Good point."

•••

A plant shelf? Unbelievable! What type of evil sadist had designed this bathroom?

Hot water beat down on Sage as she stood immobilized in her shower staring in horror at the plant-filled ledge above her bathroom door. She'd been so busy scanning the floors and walls for reptiles yesterday and again today, she hadn't noticed the artistic niche that provided the perfect location for a reptilian ambush.

Awesome.

She rolled her eyes and tried to relax. After returning from her horseback-riding excursion that day, she'd avoided Pax by having dinner delivered to her room again. She would have preferred to avoid her jungle-loving shower as well, but she didn't want to go to bed smelling like a horse.

Sage had been doing okay and almost enjoying the shower when she'd noticed the plant shelf above the door. Now every time she walked into her bathroom, she had to worry about a slithering snake pouncing onto her head.

Holy buckets! Something had moved up there.

Without taking her eyes from the plant in question, she turned off the shower, grabbed her towel, and secured it around her body with a knot above her breasts. Unless she wanted to scramble over the unfinished wall of her shower, the door directly under the ledge provided her only way of escape. Should she hurdle the wall, tiptoe quietly from the bathroom, or make a run for it?

A little green head with two beady eyes peeked through the leaves at her, and her feet made the decision for her. She bolted out of the shower, through her bathroom, and straight out of the villa's front door into the moonlit night.

Dripping wet and panting, she stood on the wooden deck. She took a number of deep breaths, and then for good measure she took a few more. Just as she started to regain control, the image of those shallow, soulless eyes flashed in her mind, sparking an involuntary leg kick and a whole-body shiver. "Stupid gecko!"

"Need any help?"

Sage yelped at the sound of Pax's voice. Of course he'd be the one to see her here, looking like a fool. She raised her head to find him no more than twenty feet away, grinning at her. When she looked closer, she realized it was more than a grin—the bastard was fighting back laughter.

"Nope. I'm completely fine." She'd be damned if she would ask him to save her. "Just enjoying that little extra touch of nature your resort provides." She clenched her teeth as she slicked her soaking hair from her face.

This time he did laugh, a deep bark of laughter that shot off annoyingly attractive golden sparks in his liquid brown eyes. He walked up the steps to her villa, still grinning as he strolled past her and through the open door. When he returned a few minutes later, hands cupped together in front of him, she instinctively shied away. With a casual grace, Pax leaned over the railing of the deck and released a small green lizard onto the branch of a tree.

"Your little visitor is harmless. See, he's gone now." He stepped closer. "Susanna said you had dinner delivered to your villa again. I thought I should check to make sure everything is okay."

"I'm fine," she lied. "I have some work to catch up on, that's all."

He looked at her with a raised eyebrow. "Alright. Then I'll let you finish your shower."

"Wait." She shot her arm out like one of those little exit gates at a parking garage, but she misjudged her aim. Her hand landed on his rock solid chest. Right about nipple level, in fact.

For a very long second, they both froze.

Then she ripped her hand away. "I'm sorry... I mean, thank you. Thank you for getting the lizard. Not thank you for letting me cop a feel." She cringed, seemingly powerless to stop the nervous rambling. "Not that I meant to cop a feel, that was an accident. Sorry for that. And thank you for the lizard. Yep, thank you and sorry. Oh, and I hate that stupid shower." She bit down on her bottom lip to physically prevent the ridiculous spew of words coming from her mouth.

"You're the one who inspired the open concept."

"What are you talking about?"

"The night by the pool—when you insisted on a shower before you swam—you told me you loved showering surrounded by nature." Pax's voice was as thick as smoke. "I never forgot it."

Sage drew in a sharp breath and felt the knot on her towel slip loose. A strangled sound escaped her throat as she grabbed the fabric an instant before

61

their little encounter earned an R rating. She clutched the towel hard. His gaze dropped to her fisted hand, and his eyes went dark.

"I'm as bad as Logan," he mumbled.

"What?"

"Nothing." He shook his head and turned to leave.

"Thanks again for the rescue."

"Any time."

"It won't happen again," she murmured to herself, pushing back a wave of desire when her wayward gaze dropped to admire his very fine butt as he strode away.

The memories he'd brought up from the past had triggered a crystal-clear solution to her current problem. She needed reinforcements, and she knew just who to call.

SEVEN

"WOW! This place is gorgeous. I'm glad I brought my big suitcase. I just might stay awhile."

At the sound of her best friend's voice in the hacienda's lobby, Sage sagged back in her chair in relief. After the charged incident with Pax the evening before, she'd called Katherine Bennett, and her wonderfully impulsive friend had arrived in less than twenty-four hours.

Okay, she'd fibbed a little to get Kat there so quickly. Telling Pax's sister that he really seemed to miss his family and that it would be a great (big!) surprise for him if Kat came to visit was a dirty trick to play on Pax. But desperate times and all that. Sage needed a buffer for the remainder of the week, and vivacious Kat fit the bill perfectly. Plus, Sage hoped the trip would be good for Kat who'd seemed distracted and a little lost ever since quitting her job in DC and moving home with her parents five months ago.

"I'll be right there," Sage called toward the lobby as she lowered her laptop's screen and quickly gathered the papers spread about the table in front of her. Since breakfast, she'd been studying La Vida's financial records in Pax's office. After the dubious horseback riding excursion yesterday, she needed both time and space from Pax while she waited for the cavalry to arrive.

After a quick review of the records, any concern she'd harbored that Pax's resort would prove to be financially unsound disappeared quicker than her first cup of morning coffee. Over the past five years, La Vida continually showed strong, reliable profits—most of which had been reinvested back into the resort.

If Pax had more money to put down on the loan, his request would be a no-brainer. But she understood why the bank was hesitant to hold the vast majority of the mortgage. If Pax grew tired of La Vida, he could walk away with little to no financial loss. In her gut, she knew he'd never do that, but she doubted the bank would ignore its own safety measures on account of her gut's opinion.

Pax loved this place. He'd be crushed if he had to let it go. And what would that make her if his loan was denied? The evil stepmother of the banking industry? The destroyer of dreams?

"What a mess," she muttered, shaking off the ominous thought as she headed to the lobby and hugged the petite brunette standing in the doorway. "Kat, I'm so happy you're here. I hope it wasn't too difficult to get away on short notice."

"No problem at all." Kat hugged her back. "I quit. My boss was a jackass anyway."

Horrified, and a little impressed, Sage stepped back and gawked at her friend. Leaving work early on a Friday made Sage nervous. She would never be able to quit a job without having an even better one lined up. "You quit? What did you say?"

"I said the job blowed and that he was a terrible boss. I threw in a few curse words for good measure," Kat said with a grin. "But I know you don't like it when I swear, so I'll stick to the edited version for you."

"I don't mind if you swear within reason. I only cringe when you make threats that aren't physically possible to follow through on."

"But those are the best kind."

"Just try to behave around Pax, okay? He seems a little stressed right now." Sage hoped she hadn't made a mistake by inviting Kat. Even though her friend only reached a couple inches over five feet and a few pounds over a hundred, her powerhouse personality made her a force to be reckoned with.

"Where is Pax?" Kat's gaze swept the lobby, interest lighting her blue-gray eyes. "You know he's going to freak when he realizes a beloved member of his family has invaded his private oasis. We've all wanted to land an invitation for years, and he's always missed our subtle hints."

"I don't know how to break this to you, Kat, but you've never, ever been subtle. I'm fairly sure he ignored all of your not-so-subtle hints."

Kat tossed a smug grin over her shoulder as she glided through the lobby on light feet.

All the Bennetts moved with an inherent feline grace. Pax stalked like a predatory big cat, bringing to mind a sleek, muscular jaguar. Petite Kat's fluid, agile manner more resembled a lynx.

"I still can't believe he's trying to buy this place," Kat said. "I always thought he'd eventually move back to Silver Bay."

Sage shrugged. "He seems to love it here." She walked to the hand-carved bar that held carafes of iced juices, water, and tea. She poured two iced teas and joined Kat on the tiled deck surrounding the pool.

They sat at a sunny table between the hacienda and the pool. Two other guests—a middle-aged couple in coordinating floral swimwear—were sunning on lounge chairs near the end of the infinity pool. Across from them, a woman with pixie-cut gray hair sat at a table with her feet kicked up, eyes focused on her e-reader. The rest of the guests were either on excursions, at the beach, or enjoying their own private villas.

La Vida's records showed it ran at near-full capacity all year. When you combined the resort's spacious grounds with the fact that only sixteen guests could stay there at a time, it never felt crowded. Instead, Sage felt like she was the personal guest at a friend's tropical paradise. Since Pax and the other employees obviously considered La Vida their home, her impression seemed close to the truth.

"How's your mom?" Kat asked.

"New guy. New job. Same old story." Sage sipped her tea. "Other than that, I don't have any details. You know how it goes. My mother never has time to talk to me when she's dating somebody new. I'll hear from her once the dramatic break-up hits. Then she likes to share all the gory details."

"Ugh. How do you put up with her?"

"She's my mom. I love her even if she's immature and a bit self-centered."

"A bit?" Kat asked, an eyebrow arched.

Sage sighed. "Fine. More than a bit. It's okay. I accepted a long time ago that our relationship would never be a traditional one."

"If it helps, traditional parental relationships can suck too. My family is the epitome of traditional and look at Pax and Dad." Kat shook her head. "I can't remember the last time they said more than a few words to each other. It's gotten so bad, Pax doesn't even come home for Mom's birthday anymore."

"He's still mad that Pax didn't want to take over the family business?" Sage asked, shoving away thoughts of what happened the last time Pax visited Silver Bay for his mother's birthday.

"Yep. He can't believe the son of Richard Bennett enjoys doing menial labor at a 'two-bit motel.' His words, not mine. Dad's devoted his life to turning Bennett Industries into a household name, and even though Claire works with him everyday in the office, that's not enough. He wants the legacy to continue in the hands of his only son."

Sage had known Richard Bennett for years. While he could be stern and stubborn, he could also be incredibly kind and generous to those he loved. Surely, if he knew of La Vida's success, he would be proud of Pax? A flash of inspiration and a glimmer of hope instantly brightened her mood. Maybe Richard would even be proud enough to loan Pax the money he needed. If that happened, La Vida would be saved, and Sage could avoid becoming the grim reaper of dreams. And, more importantly, she could return to the safety of Wisconsin before something really horrible happened like getting attacked by a snake, or worse, throwing herself at Pax only to be rejected by him. Again.

Sage swallowed hard. She couldn't let either of those things happen. The faster she helped Pax and his dad mend fences, the faster she could get out of there. It wouldn't be easy, but she had an idea where to start. Problem was, Pax wouldn't like her idea.

Not even a little bit.

•••

What the hell? The sight of his little sister sitting with Sage by the pool stopped Pax dead in his tracks. How long had he been gone?

When Kat spotted him, she leapt from her chair, flew into the lobby, and threw herself onto him. "I love your home! I've decided to move here too!"

Stunned by the sudden body slam, Pax wrapped his arms around her more out of instinct than intent.

He and Logan had been at a meeting with the local school to discuss the next stage of the school's renovation. He'd been anxious to return to La Vida and had done a terrible job maintaining focus during the meeting.

Apparently, he should have focused more on what Sage was up to too.

"Kat, what the hell are you doing here?"

"Sage called me yesterday, worried about you. She said you really seemed to be missing your family, and that she thought I should fly down right away to see you. I'm going to stay in her room the rest of the week. But I'm considering moving into your place for a few months after that." Kat dropped back to the ground and laid a reassuring hand on his chest. "I think this will work out great for both of us."

A few feet behind him, he heard Logan choking back laughter.

Kat leaned around Pax and narrowed her eyes at the Australian. "Is something funny, big guy?"

"No, darl." Logan extended his hand in greeting. "I'm Logan, one of La Vida's guides."

An unreadable emotion flashed briefly across Kat's face. Ignoring Logan's outstretched hand, she scanned him up and down. "You're ridiculously large," she snapped with uncharacteristic rudeness.

"Thank you, darl."

Kat's eyes flared. "It wasn't a compliment."

"It's never been a *complaint*," Logan said, his tone full of humor and arrogance.

Warning bells went off in Pax's head. He purposely stepped between his friend and his sister. "Logan, shut the hell up. You're talking to my baby sister." He narrowed his eyes at Sage. "In my office. Now."

Her wide-eyed expression betrayed her nervousness. Good. She should be nervous—he was going to eat her alive.

"I need to let Kat into my villa," Sage croaked, scrambling to her feet. "I'm sure she wants to get settled. Isn't that right, Kat?"

"I'll show her to your villa," Logan offered, picking up Kat's luggage. "In fact, I'm happy to give you a tour of the whole resort."

Pax's blood pressure kicked up a notch. He needed to have a little talk with his friend about keeping his hands off his sister during her short stay at La Vida.

"I can take care of myself." Kat jerked her luggage out of Logan's hand. "Just show me the way."

Pax's nerves eased. It seemed Kat already knew better than to get involved with a player like Logan.

"What the hell did you say to Kat?" Pax demanded as he and Sage stepped into his office. "She's threatening to move here."

"Well, yes, that was unexpected," Sage conceded. "In my defense, I never suggested she relocate. I only said she should come for a short visit. I thought it would be fun to have her here with me."

"Fun?" Pax growled. "She's a pain in the ass."

"She isn't a pain. She's enthusiastic. No matter what you say, I know you love her, and she loves you too." Sage paused. "Plus, she misses you. Your whole family does."

He blew out a breath, guilt and frustration gnawing at his gut. "Fine. It looks like I don't have a choice about Kat, but I don't want any more of my family invited. Understood?"

"Yes." She bit her lip and looked away.

Oh, boy. He knew that look. "What?"

"I've been thinking about your loan request?"

"And?"

"While La Vida's numbers are very solid, you don't have much money to put down on the loan. Can you convince the owner to hold off selling until you have more money saved?"

"I tried, but Charlie wants out. There is no way he's going to turn down the large amount of money that damn hotel chain offered him."

"How did you get involved with Charlie in the first place?"

"I met him when I visited Costa Rica during spring break of my sophomore year at Northwestern. I was here for fun, and he'd just finished up a career in the Peace Corps. When he talked about the experiences he'd had over the years, I was awed by the sacrifices he'd made in his own life to help others." Pax moved to sit behind his desk and gestured for Sage to sit as well. "I'd never wanted the life my father had chosen for me. I liked working with my hands, building things. I didn't want to sit inside all day where business deals were the only thing I could make."

Sage nodded. "I can't imagine you in a tie."

"Just thinking about it makes me itch." Pax rubbed the back of his neck and blew out a sigh. "Charlie and I talked about the feasibility of opening a luxury resort that offered both a place to get away from the stresses of everyday life and a place to give back to others. Over the course of a few nights and a few bottles of beer, La Vida de Ensueño was born."

That week had changed his life. Before then, he'd been a wealthy kid attending a prestigious college, being groomed against his will to take over the family business. After that week, he'd quit college and joined the ranks of the working class, earning every dollar in his pocket and every callous on his hands.

"Charlie had inherited enough money from his parents to bankroll the building of La Vida, and I worked as the hands-on manager on-site. I didn't care that he owned the resort. I just wanted her to become something special. And she has."

"But?" Sage prompted.

Pax sat forward in his chair. "But Charlie moved home and now he's lost interest. He wants out. That's where your loan comes into play."

Sage looked at him with a hesitant expression. "What about your parents? The amount you need for a down payment is less money than they spent on their new boat last year. Have you considered asking them for the loan?"

He raised an eyebrow. "My father never accepted that I dropped out of college and moved here. He didn't go so far as to disown me, but let's just say he has mentioned, multiple times, what a spectacular disappointment I am. If I went to him for money now, he would laugh in my face as he told me no."

"You don't know that," Sage argued. "If you had bothered to visit more often, you would realize your father has mellowed over the last few years. I can tell he misses you like everyone else does. And if you weren't such a stubborn ass, you'd realize that facing the past issues you've had with your dad, rather than hiding from them, could be the answer to all of your problems." She glared at him for a moment longer, then stormed out of his office.

Pax let out a groan and wondered why the hell the bank couldn't have sent a normal loan officer? Some guy named Bill, who liked to wear brown suits, boring ties, and who knew absolutely nothing about Pax's personal life.

Karma really was a bitch.

EIGHT

"YOU'VE been frowning at those poor clothes so long I'm afraid you're going to give them a complex," Kat said from the doorway of the villa's bedroom.

Stationed in front of her suitcase for the past fifteen minutes, Sage had considered every possible outfit option. "I've eaten in my room the past two nights. This will be my first time having dinner at the hacienda with everyone else. I'm not sure what to wear."

"Pick something. I'm hungry. I'll be waiting on the couch."

Sage rolled her eyes and snatched a pair of trim white pants and a light pink, three-quarter-sleeve silk top. The outfit would have to do. Although the breezy top had a deep vee in the front, she considered the amount of cleavage it showed flirty rather than skanky. She added dangly earrings, a silver cuff bracelet, and nude, peep-toe platform pumps. She secured her hair into a twist and finished the look with a sheer lip gloss and a smoky eye.

"Okay, I'm ready to go," she told Kat as she stepped into the villa's main room.

Kat took one look at Sage and gave an exaggerated sigh. "Why do you tall girls insist on wearing heels? You make it impossible for the rest of us to keep up. And, frankly, I'm tired of playing Skipper to your Barbie."

Sage laughed. "Trust me, no one thinks of you as Barbie's younger sister." She eyed her friend's black slim-fitting pants, stretchy tank top, and slicked-back ponytail. "With all the black you're wearing, you're more likely to be mistaken for Lara Croft, exotic locale and all."

"I'll take that as a compliment. Lara Croft kicks ass." Kat smirked. "Let's go. I haven't seen Pax in a couple hours. He's probably missing me."

Doubtful. More likely Pax would rather both Kat and Sage pulled a no-show.

Towering over Kat on the walk to the hacienda, Sage began to question her shoe choice. The moment she stepped onto the tiled pool deck and her gaze locked on to Pax, she thanked the stars for her added height.

He was leaning casually against the wooden bar with a beer in his hand, talking to the floral-print couple she'd seen at the pool earlier. He wore dark jeans and an untucked black button-down shirt with the sleeves rolled to his elbows. He'd shaved tonight which gave him the mouthwatering appearance of being both rugged and polished.

He looked up, caught her staring, and gave her a look so intense that she would have run away if Kat hadn't been by her side.

"Hey, Brick," Sage said, ignoring Pax. "Are you La Vida's bartender too?"

"I help out a few nights a week." He wiped the spot in front of them with a towel. "It's a great way to meet the guests."

When she introduced Kat, his eyes went wide. "Pax has never had family here before. I was beginning to think he'd made up the whole bunch of you."

This coming from the king of exaggerated stories.

"I think I might move here," Kat said cheerfully.

"Sweet! Now, what can I get you ladies to drink?" Brick asked. "If you're not sure, I recommend a mojito. I use Gloria Estefan's personal recipe."

Sage grinned. "A mojito sounds lovely." No doubt he had a story to go with that recipe—one full of entertainment and creativity that likely featured Brick as a former backup dancer for Ms. Estefan.

"Make that two," Kat chimed in.

A few minutes later, mojito in hand, Sage heard Susanna's raised voice.

"Did I just hear the words 'hopeless' and 'ass' coming from the kitchen?" Kat asked, eyebrows raised. She took a sip of her drink.

Sage laughed. "That's Susanna, the matronly chef with an iron fist. I have a pretty good idea who she's chastising in there. Let's check it out." She scooped up her drink and led the way into the spacious kitchen.

Kitchen staff were hard at work, using all available surfaces and appliances. At the far end of the scene, at a counter near the industrial-sized oven, Susanna glared at Logan. The big Australian had an egg in his hand and a hesitant look on his face. He tapped the egg way too gently against a mixing bowl and then examined it for any cracks.

"No! You are doing it wrong. Do it like this." Susanna snatched the egg from his hand, cracked it against the countertop, and expertly emptied it into the mixing bowl. "I swear, Logan, I gave you the easiest dessert recipe and you are still hopeless."

"Come on, darl, give me a break. I'm not a baker." Logan turned on a smile so full of charm Sage imagined it had gotten him laid many times in the past. "I can't even read this paper. What's a 't-s-p'?"

Ouch. Sage winced and watched Susanna's face redden like cartoon smoke was about to come out of her ears. Instead, a rush of angry-sounding Spanish came pouring out of the chef's mouth.

"Whoa. Señora Pineda never taught those words in Spanish class," Kat said.

"I thought the same thing yesterday," Sage whispered. "Logan wined, dined, and dumped Susanna's last two pastry chefs. I assume this is his punishment. Come on. This is too painful to watch. Let's see if we can help."

Sage dragged Kat to the back wall and dropped aprons around both of their necks. She pulled Kat over to the war zone and directed her friendliest smile at the simmering chef. "Kat and I would like to help Logan make the dessert tonight. Would that be okay with you?"

Susanna shifted her narrowed eyes at Sage. "That depends. Do you know what a 't-s-p' is?"

"Yes. I also know the difference between a 't-s-p' and a 't-b-s-p.' I love to bake," Sage said. "But don't worry, I'll make sure Logan has work to do, as well."

Susanna stared her down for a tension-filled minute. "Fine. You are in charge, but don't let him off too easy. He needs to learn the cost of his dallying."

Once the chef moved out of range, Logan let out a sigh. "Thanks, Sage. She scares me."

"Don't be ridiculous. She couldn't hurt you," Kat said in a clipped voice. She stared blankly at the space Susanna had just filled.

"What's wrong?" Sage whispered, surprised by her friend's tone and her unusually dark expression.

Kat shook her head, breaking the trance. "I'm fine. Now let's get to work before the mean lady comes back."

•••

Two hours and two contraband mojitos later, they finished taking the last individual chocolate lava cakes from the oven. While Sage and Kat had done all of the real cooking, Logan had helped with the simple tasks, including sneaking the extra mojitos into Susanna's kitchen and risking the return of her rage.

Sage held her breath as Susanna inspected the cakes like a general inspecting her troops. Sage hadn't lied—she had always loved to bake. She found it a relaxing way to express her rarely called upon creative side. Honestly, the recipe had been very easy. If she found a little free time this week, she might stop back in the kitchen and try her hand at a more difficult one.

Finally, Susanna nodded her head in affirmation. "You three did good. Now sit. Eat." She gestured to the large kitchen table, set with six mouthwatering plates of food.

"Is it safe to come in there?" Brick's voice boomed from the entryway.

Kat laughed. "Don't worry, you chicken. The work's all done."

Brick crossed the room and joined Sage, Kat, Susanna, and Logan at the table to enjoy the fish Susanna had prepared.

"Where's Pax?" Kat asked.

"He's trapped talking to some guests," Brick said, leaning across the table to grab a slice of bread. "They love him. A group of ladies stayed here last month, and they couldn't get enough of Pax. Poor guy had to hide at his house in the evenings to avoid the unwanted attention."

"Poor guy?" Kat scoffed. "Pax probably loves having women dropping at his feet."

"Depends on the woman." A faint smile played around Pax's mouth as he walked into the kitchen, his gaze locked on Sage.

"That's your problem, mate. You're too picky." Logan picked up the open bottle of California Cabernet on the table, poured a glass for Pax, then set it down at the empty place setting next to Sage.

Susanna's eyes narrowed. "And you, Logan, could make all of our lives easier by being a little more picky."

"Come on, darl, don't be a wowser."

The older woman's face reddened in anger. "Wowser? That better be Australian for an intelligent woman."

Sage's gaze ping-ponged between the two.

"My money is on Susanna," Pax murmured near her ear. "Logan's got her in size, but she's a lot more spirited."

"Shouldn't you stop them?"

"They need to work through this on their own. I'll step in if any blood is shed."

"You sound like a parent," she teased.

Pax blew out a long, slow breath. "You have no idea how many times I feel like the head of a very dysfunctional family."

"Susie, he didn't mean no harm. He's just fooling around, right?" Brick turned to Logan, taking on the role of the peacemaking middle child.

"Good-o." Logan smiled, looking pleased with himself.

Susanna stared Logan down for a full five seconds before turning her attention to the half-eaten plates on the table. "Eat. All of you. Before the food is ruined."

After finishing the delicious meal, Sage relaxed back in her chair and sipped her glass of wine. She'd never been a big drinker, and after two mojitos, she should probably take it easy on the wine.

Her lowered defenses allowed in a depressing jolt of epiphany. Her life had turned out very differently than Pax's. Though he had chosen an unconventional path, people who loved and respected Pax surrounded him. In contrast, she'd always played it safe—followed the rules—and at the end of the week, she would be returning to a relatively empty life.

"What's wrong?" Pax's voice broke into her thoughts.

"I was thinking about home," she said, which was true. "I, ah, can't remember if I paid my cable bill this month. It's due tomorrow." Okay, that wasn't true. She paid her cable bill on the first day of every month. But she wasn't ready to fess up her real concern that her life might be a little empty, boring even.

Pax pulled his mobile phone from his pocket and placed it on the table in front of her. "Use my phone to check. I know you'll worry until you do."

"Thanks," she mumbled, oddly touched by his gesture. He knew she would worry about paying a bill late, even for nonessential cable. She liked that he didn't make fun of her concern or tell her not to worry about such trivial things.

Kat rose from the table and extended her hand toward Sage. "Come on lady, let's go for a swim before heading back to the villa."

"Pool or ocean?" Sage asked.

"Ocean, of course. We can swim in a pool anywhere."

"No way." Sage shook her head slowly from side to side. "Sharks feed at night."

"You're afraid of sharks now?" Pax asked, the corner of his lips twitching slightly.

Sage narrowed her eyes at him. "Don't you dare laugh. Fear is a completely natural response to the possibility of becoming a great white's yummy snack."

"Come on, Sage, I don't want to go alone," Kat pleaded.

"I'll swim with you," Logan offered with a mischievous smile.

"No, you won't," Pax snapped then turned to Kat. "If you insist on going, I'll go with you."

"Fine," Kat huffed, "but now I can't skinny dip."

Pax grimaced and stood up from the table. "I'll walk both you and Sage back to her villa. You can put your suit on there."

Sage shook her head. "No thanks. I'm fine here with Logan. Make sure you remember to change this time," she told Pax, and then explained, "Pax has been known to jump into the water fully clothed."

"Let's go, big brother." Kat slugged an exasperated looking Pax on the shoulder as she hurried from the room.

Logan leaned across the table and filled Sage's wine glass to the brim. "Better run along, mate. Need to watch out for your sister."

Pax's eyes darkened as he shifted his gaze from Logan to the wine glass and then back to Logan again. He scowled at the big Australian.

"Don't worry about Sage." Logan winked. "I'll look after *her*."

For a long, tense minute, Pax lasered a death glare at him. Then he stormed from the room, muttering a colorful phrase that Sage tried to reserve for truly painful moments, like stubbing her toe or bikini waxes.

Amusement lit Logan's eyes. "No worries. He just said he has 'somewhat of an itch.'"

Sage swallowed a snort. "Oh, really? I thought he called you a son of a—"

"It's such a lovely night, darl," Logan interrupted with an easy smile. "Let's move to a table outside." He pushed back his chair and made a lead-the-way gesture.

"Great idea." Sage was happy to extend the enjoyable evening. She slipped Pax's phone into her pocket and took a quick gulp of wine, lowering its near overflowing level so it didn't slosh out while she carried it in her ever-so-slightly inebriated state.

She carefully strolled from the kitchen, through the hacienda, and onto the patio surrounding the pool, thankful the relaxing effect of the wine hadn't hampered her ability to walk in heels. She only stumbled twice. Well, maybe three times, but she was pretty sure it didn't count if no-one else saw her do it. She plopped down at a table for two, looking out over the moonlit ocean beyond.

Logan sat beside her, stretched his long legs in front of him, and sipped from his own glass of wine. A comfortable silence settled around them. Well, not quite silence. Even at night, songs of animals and insects mixed with the distant ocean waves, enveloping the night in tranquility.

Eventually, Sage felt Logan's gaze on her. "Are you going to give him the loan?" he asked.

Sage considered her words carefully, at least as carefully as possible after multiple drinks. "I emailed my preliminary report earlier today, but I don't have the final say."

"Did you recommend the loan?"

"I gave an honest report on the resort's financial standings as well as a detailed report of the grounds and the activities offered."

"How come it sounds like you're dancing around my question?"

She blew out her breath, deflating both her posture and her attempt at being professional. "My gut says he won't get the loan. The bank wants him to have more money to put down on the place. I don't think they'll overlook his lack of funding just because I said it's great here."

"Pax deserves this place. Is there anything else you can do?"

"Maybe." She slipped Pax's phone from her pocket.

Logan looked at the phone and then back at her. "Do I want to know?"

"Probably not." She turned it on, not sure if it was good or bad that she didn't need a password. Maybe it was a sign. She shrugged and quickly did what needed to be done and put the phone away before she could think about the consequences. "Done."

"Good-o. So, are you going to tell me the real story between you and Pax?"

"Nope," she answered, turning to look at him. "Are you going to tell me the real reason you made Pax think you planned to hit on me when you had no intention of doing so?"

The corners of Logan's mouth turned up in a crooked grin. "Sure," he answered. "I've never seen him so worked up about a woman before."

"Have there been a lot of woman for him to get worked up about?" Sage asked, shooting for nonchalance. "Sounds like some of the female guests have been interested in him before."

"He's not a saint if that's what you're asking. But he's never been serious about anyone here, and he'd never mess around with a guest. Got to say though, he might break that rule for you. I've never seen him look at a woman like that before."

She gulped. "How does he look at me?" She remembered Pax asking her a similar question that long-ago night by the pool in Silver Bay.

"Like he..." Logan's voice trailed off and his grin widened.

"Go on," Sage said, gesturing for him to talk.

"On second thought, if you don't already know, then you should probably ask Pax."

She scowled at him. "Fine. Be unhelpful. But that still doesn't explain why you pretended to hit on me."

"I like pissing Pax off, and there's obviously something between you two." He gave a careless shrug. "Wanted to see how he would react."

Sage shook her head. "I'll never understand why guys like to be jerks to each other."

"It's just what we do," he said with a wink. "I'll let you in on a secret, as long as you promise not to tell him."

"Deal."

"Pax is like a brother to me. I'd never actually let a woman come between us."

"That may be the nicest thing I've ever heard one guy say about another." Sage leaned close and placed her palm over his heart. "You have a big heart, Logan McCabe."

Logan looked up and froze. "Darl, would you be kind enough to move your hand? I might like pissing

Pax off, but right now I'm starting to fear for my life."

Sage followed Logan's line of sight. Pax stood silently at the top of the path leading from the beach, eyes as black as the night around him.

"Hey, mate. Done with your swim, ay?" Jumping to his feet, Logan shoved his hands in the front pockets of his jeans.

"Kat changed her mind," he growled.

"Guess I'll be heading back to my place and give you two old friends time to catch up," Logan said, backing away.

"Chicken," Sage mouthed.

With a devilish grin, Logan bolted.

She cocked her head and squinted at Pax. He looked pissed. Really pissed. Or maybe tired? Frustrated? Maybe all three? She couldn't quite tell, and to be honest, the lovely mojito-wine buzz made it hard to catch her thoughts right now. Like snowflakes falling on a winter day, they were floating around in her head, but if she tried to grip one too hard, poof! It was gone.

She squinted a little more, imagining his eyes were full of passion rather than anger. Damn, he looked good. Her blood started to heat. "Do you want to make out? You know, for old times' sake?"

"Damn it, Sage. You're killing me here." His voice rumbled from his throat as he strode toward her, and for one blissful moment, she thought he was going to kiss her. Instead, he stormed past her and disappeared into the brightly lit hacienda.

Okay, that's not how the scene had played out in her head. Sure, somewhere in her hazy mind, a thought nagged that making out with Pax was a bad idea. But right now, it seemed like the best idea she'd had since arriving in Costa Rica.

She stood, determined to find him before enough rational thought returned to ruin the fun. Before she moved from the table, however, he was back, placing a bottle of water into her hand.

"Drink up. You'll thank me in the morning."

She sidled closer. "I'd rather thank you for something else in the morning."

"You're drunk."

"Tipsy. There's a difference. I haven't been drunk since my first week of college. It was horrible. My head spun, and all I wanted to do was sleep. Or barf. When I'm tipsy, I'm a lot more fun." She emphasized her words with a playful wink.

"Shit," Pax muttered with a pained expression, rubbing the back of his neck. "I feel like a damn camp counselor. I have to lifeguard Kat and babysit you."

"What's the big deal? We've kissed before." Sage tiptoed her fingers up his chest.

"You might want to lower your voice," Pax growled in her ear, grabbing her wrist. "Or do you want the entire resort to know the details of our past?" He eyed the guests enjoying an evening cocktail at the bar on the other side of the hacienda's lobby.

"There's not much to know. You said no," she said, flinging her free arm in frustration. "Seriously, Pax? What guy turns down sex?"

Cursing under his breath, he hustled her away from the pool and steered her silently down the dimly lit path to her villa. He guided her up to the private deck facing the ocean and then dropping his grip on her wrist. Turning, he braced his hands on the deck's railing and faced the ocean rather than her.

"What, nothing to say?" Sage asked, carefully placing her bottle of water on the railing, a few feet away from him. "Just like you had nothing to say then."

"I was returning to Costa Rica in a few days," he said, his voice low and frustrated. "Having sex with you would not have been a good idea."

"Good idea or not, it was damn embarrassing to be turned down when I wanted you so much." She threw the words at him. "I still feel like an idiot every time I think about that night."

"Sage—"

"No." She shook her head, unable to stand the pity in his voice. "No. Forget I said anything. I don't want to talk about this."

Pax moved down the rail toward her, stopping so close she could feel the heat from his body and smell the spicy scent of his skin. Against her better judgment, she drew in a long breath and moaned, leaning into him. Pax still pushed her past reason.

"I wanted you," he rasped, his voice raw. "I still do." He tilted up her chin and brushed his lips gently across hers. "Sage," he murmured, wrapping his arms around her and molding her body to his.

His tenderness set off a rush of emotion in her chest.

She parted her lips, and Pax deepened the kiss, slowly, thoroughly exploring her mouth as his hands caressed her. Her body tightened and desire swirled through, ending in an ache low in her belly.

"Let's go inside," she coaxed between kisses.

His mouth stilled on hers. "Kat's inside taking a shower."

"Then take me to your place."

"This still isn't a good idea."

"It feels like a great idea to me."

Pax stepped away, shaking his head. "You're here on business, not for a fling. That's all this would be. I live here. You live a world away. You've made it clear you'll never change your life for a man."

"Buzzkill," Sage grumbled.

"Am I wrong?" he asked, scrubbing a hand down his face.

"No, but—"

"Goodnight, Sage," Pax interrupted, his jaw tense and his eyes hard.

And then he was gone, leaving her slightly dizzy and utterly confused.

NINE

"I'M going to be an awesome surfer! This is one time those Barbie legs aren't going to help. My lower center of gravity will make it way easier for me to balance."

Groaning at Kat's enthusiastic ramblings, Sage closed her eyes—currently hidden behind sunglasses—and laid her head against the Land Rover's backseat headrest. While not fully hungover, thanks to the water Pax had pushed on her last night, she still felt like crap this morning.

Today was surf-lesson day. No matter how much she'd pleaded, Kat wouldn't let her bail. Her friend had guilted her into coming along by reminding Sage of the over two-thousand-mile trip Kat had made for her with less than twenty-four hours' notice.

They'd left La Vida right after breakfast, Pax and Logan in the front two seats, Sage and Kat in the back, driving to a town called Talara, the best local beach for beginners to surf. Determined—desperate really—to maintain her dignity today, Sage planned to hang back and try to get her relationship with Pax back on a professional path.

Talking about her legs wasn't helping things.

"Barbie legs?" Logan questioned.

"Sage looks like Barbie. Don't act like you hadn't noticed," Kat chastised. "When she's dressed for work in her tailored suits and five inch heels, she makes the perfect Banker Barbie."

Pax grunted while Sage groaned again, wishing she were still in bed. Or back in Milwaukee. Or anywhere other than heading to a beach to spend the day with a guy she'd thrown herself at. Twice!

Pax maneuvered the SUV from the main road and headed up a street lined with colorfully painted houses. He waved to three weathered-looking grandpa types sitting on the front stoop of a bright yellow home with a small, well-maintained yard. The men dipped their heads in acknowledgement and returned a simple wave.

The farther they drove, the closer together the houses became. Eventually they gave way to a small town. Out the right side of the SUV, Sage could see glimpses of the Pacific Ocean between the beach shops, restaurants, and bars lining the main street. On the sidewalks, bathing-suit-clad tourists and locals, all loaded with beach gear, hustled to reach the crashing blue waves.

"Talara is mainly a beach town," Pax explained. "Even though surfers and other tourists found her a few years back, there are no chain hotels or high-rise condos."

Sage sat up straighter and studied the view out the window. "I like how the homes and businesses have personalities here. They're not all painted beige, white, or gray like the ones back home. They seem happy."

"Yes, but they're a lot smaller and don't have a number of luxuries found in America," Pax said. "Does that bother you?"

"Not at all," she insisted. "They're charming."

"I'm glad you think so. The visitors who take the time to actually meet some of the local residents—Ticos as they're called—quickly find out how happy the people are here. In fact, Costa Rica often ranks as the happiest country in the world."

"Seriously?" Kat asked.

"Look it up. The United States' per capita GDP is four times the size of Costa Rica's, yet Ticos report being happier than Americans."

Logan threw a devilish grin over his shoulder. "Pax is not only trying to bring the world together, he wants to teach us all that money doesn't buy happiness."

Pax made a dismissive noise. "You make me sound like a damn hippie."

"Well, I think it's great, how you encourage guests to get involved in the local area," Kat said. "I'm proud of you, big brother."

Pax stared straight ahead at the road.

"Hello?" Kat pestered. "Did you hear me?"

"Yeah. Thanks," he mumbled.

Sage hesitated, recognizing Pax's discomfort at talking about himself. Too bad for him. This was her chance to take care of Ann's dubious assignment once and for all. "So, Pax, are you happy in Costa Rica?"

"Is that so hard to believe?"

"No. Not to nitpick, though, but you didn't answer my question."

Pax huffed out a sigh. "Yeah. I'm happy here. Happier than I was or ever could be in Wisconsin."

Like it or not, she had her answer. Sage could now report back to Ann that her son had built a good life, a happy life, in Costa Rica. Since Pax had always made it clear he had no plans to return to Wisconsin, his contentment in Costa Rica was a good thing.

So what did the ache of disappointment suspiciously near Sage's heart say about her?

"We're here." Pax pulled into a tiny gravel parking lot in front of a shop sporting a large, decorative longboard over the door. A hand-written sign advertising surf lessons hung in the window. He climbed from the vehicle, opened the back door for Sage, and extended his hand to her.

"How are you feeling this morning?" he asked, his voice low enough for only her to hear.

"A little sluggish and a lot embarrassed," she admitted with a sigh. She climbed out slowly, stalling to give Kat and Logan time to enter the building ahead of them. She didn't want an audience when she gave the speech she'd planned in her head.

Pax didn't move toward the shop either. His gaze locked with hers. The intensity of his expression combined with the scent of soap rising from his warm skin almost made Sage lightheaded. She turned away and drew in another breath, filling her lungs with the salty ocean air.

She kept her gaze on the distant water. "Two drinks is usually my limit. I'm sorry you had to deal with me well past that point."

"We've all misjudged our limits." Pax paused. "But you'll want to back off of Logan. He's not your type."

Now that ticked her off. The man who'd repeatedly turned down her sexual advances, albeit not well-thought-out ones, was now giving advice on her love life? Unbelievable. So what if Logan wasn't her type? So what if she hadn't actually been flirting with him? It might be good for Pax to know the possibility existed that she could be attracted to someone else.

"Oh, really?" she drawled. "He's a sweet, good-looking guy who's built like a—"

"Are you making a point?" Pax growled.

"My point is," she continued, "I'm free to be with anyone I want."

"What about Will?"

Holy buckets. What kind of horrible person was she? She hadn't thought about Will in two days. It didn't matter that she'd gone out with him only four times. Before she'd left Milwaukee, she'd definitely planned on seeing him again. Yet Pax had distracted her to the point of amnesia. Damn him for remembering what she'd so easily forgotten.

She narrowed her eyes. "We've only been out a few times. We're both free to see other people."

"I thought you had a promising future planned with the banker. Flirting with Logan could risk all that."

"Seemed like a good idea at the time." She shrugged, not bothering to explain that she hadn't been flirting with Logan.

Pax stepped toward her. "A good idea? It seemed like a good idea to hit on a guy twice your size?" He

93

took another step closer, backing her against the black SUV. "What would you have done if he'd accepted your offer? What if, even right now, he regrets telling you no?"

"Are we still talking about Logan?" She tipped her chin up. "Or are you finally getting tired of rejecting me all the time?"

"Rejecting you?" He leaned back, eyebrows raised. "Damn it, Sage, is that what you think?"

"You keep walking away."

His jaw tensed and his expression filled with emotions—heat, anger, frustration. "The two times I walked away I did it for your own good. But I'm not a saint." He leaned closer to her, his voice dropping to a murmur. "The next time, I won't walk away, even if I should. Understood?"

"Yep," she squeaked.

He ran a rough hand through his hair and sighed. A big, full-bodied thing that left no doubt how frustrating he currently found her. "I'll see you inside," he said as he strode past her into the surf shop.

Trying to get her heart rate under control, she sagged against the SUV and again wondered about the question that plagued her. Why did she have to be so insanely attracted to a man whose life and future were thousands of miles away from her own?

•••

Twenty minutes later, Sage stood on the beach dressed in her bright-blue boy-short bikini bottoms and a black midriff-baring wetsuit top. The top had long-sleeves, a full zipper, and was on loan from the surf shop. Next to her, dressed in a similar outfit but in all black, Kat stood on top of a surfboard on the beach pretending to ride a wave into shore.

Kat eyed the ocean with enthusiasm. "Enough talk. Let's hit the water."

Being La Vida's best surfer, Logan had given them a brief lesson on how to mount the board and surf to shore. Sage now had a basic understanding and a mild desire to attempt surfing, but she still lacked Kat's eagerness to "shoot the curl," whatever the heck that meant.

Logan's gaze was locked on Kat and lit up with amusement. "Okay, Gidget, hop off your board. I'll carry it out for you."

"Gidget!" Kat roared, shoving at Logan in a futile attempt to push him away as he bent to pick up her board. "Unless you want your boys relocated to your throat, do not call me Gidget!" Eyes blazing, Kat scooped up her surfboard, tucked it under her arm, and stomped off toward the ocean.

Logan turned to Sage and Pax, eyebrows raised and palms up in a what-did-I-say gesture.

Sage smiled reassuringly. "Don't worry. She's never carried out one of her exaggerated threats before. She just needs a minute to cool down."

Pax shrugged. "Looks like she's immune to your charms, mate. Personally, I'm glad she hates your guts. Means I don't have to kick your ass if you touch her."

Sage rolled her eyes. Men could be such idiots. "Maybe Kat prefers not to be teased about her size." Not that her best friend had ever seemed concerned about it before.

A frown settled between Logan's eyes. "I didn't mean to hurt her feelings. I'll go apologize."

Sage made a mental note to ask her friend again what was wrong. Normally, Kat would have loved Logan's height, muscular build, and mesmerizing accent. Kat had once told Sage she'd majored in International Affairs in college because she hoped to sleep with a lot of hot foreign guys. Sure, Kat had been mostly kidding, but Sage always suspected the statement held a bit of truth.

Pax picked up Sage's surfboard, and they started toward where Kat and Logan stood talking farther down the beach.

"Logan has been with La Vida almost as long as I have," he said quietly. "He's my best friend. I'd trust him with my life." He paused, staring ahead as the big Australian tucked a strand of hair behind Kat's ear, followed immediately by Kat swatting his hand away. "But I am still glad she hates him."

Sage dug her toes in the sand and swallowed a laugh. Birds soared overhead in the cloudless sky, and the cool Pacific water rolled over her feet. A prefect tropical day. Nothing to worry about.

So why was her pulse beating so fast?

•••

After the onshore surf lesson, Pax cut through the water, determined to reach his sister before she spent much time alone with Logan. Too bad Brick couldn't surf to save his life. Better him than Logan, who too often charmed the pants off the women he met. Literally.

Pax had originally hired the Australian to give surf lessons at La Vida since Logan had grown up with a longboard under his feet. A friendship had developed quickly between the two men, and Logan's responsibilities at the resort had grown over time. Even though he liked to piss Pax off from time to time, Logan always had his back. That didn't mean, however, that Pax wanted him touching either of the two women currently wreaking havoc in his life.

"Quick review before the first go at it." Logan stood in chest-deep water, holding on to Kat's board. "I'll boost you onto your board. When I say go, start paddling toward shore, and I'll give you a push. When you feel the wave start to carry you forward, put your hands in a push-up position. Then pop your front foot directly between your hands in the middle of the board and slowly stand up."

"Got it. I'll go first," Kat said.

Logan grabbed her hips and lifted her onto the board in one effortless motion.

"Here comes a good wave. Get ready, darl. Go!" Logan commanded as he shoved Kat's board toward shore.

Kat popped to her feet, let out a shriek of excitement, and stayed upright for a good five seconds before tipping into the water. Not bad for a first timer.

"Your turn." Pax moved behind Sage, wrapping his hands firmly around the curves of her hips.

Her body tensed.

"Do you want me to let you go?" Despite the question, he instinctively tightened his hold on her smooth, slick skin.

"Maybe," she murmured, her breathing growing heavy. "I'm not sure what I want anymore."

Fighting the rush of desire to pull her against his body, he gritted his teeth and boosted her out of the water and onto her surfboard.

"I can't believe I'm saying this," Pax mumbled, struggling to clear his mind and cool his blood. "I think Logan should lift you out of the water next time."

TEN

SAGE agreed that it was probably best if Pax kept his hands to himself.

Still, by the end of the day, she felt like a pro on the water, carving waves and completing aerials with graceful ease. Well, at least that's how it felt to her. In the spirit of full disclosure, her greatest achievement was standing on the board and riding a gentle wave for almost fifteen seconds.

Surprisingly, she'd really enjoyed the three activities she'd participated in so far at La Vida. She never would have imagined horseback riding, swimming behind a waterfall, and surfing could be so much fun. She might be braver than she'd ever given herself credit for. She smiled at the satisfying thought.

Even spending time with Pax had turned out okay. As long as she and Pax avoided touching each other, they got along fine. While he gave her tips on improving her form, she teased him about making Kat the new full-time surfing instructor at La Vida.

As predicted, Kat had taken to the sport straightaway, her lean, athletic build adjusting easily to the challenge of balancing on a board rushing over the waves.

"Hi, y'all," Brick greeted them as they returned to the surf shop's parking lot. "Pax said you needed a pick up?"

"I only need you to take Logan and Kat back to La Vida," Pax said, stepping to the front of the group. "I'd like to show Sage something in town before we return."

Sage raised an eyebrow in question but didn't comment. Instead, she said a quick goodbye to Logan, Kat, and Brick and slid into the passenger side of the Land Rover. Pax climbed into the driver's seat, started the SUV, and left the parking lot, driving in the opposite direction of La Vida.

"Aren't you going to ask where we're going?"

Sage shrugged. "I trust you. Plus, I'm completely drained. Who knew surfing would be so exhausting?"

Pax grinned. "You loved it."

She laughed. "Surprisingly, I did. I'm turning into quite the adventurer. If I keep this up, my rep might be upgraded from boring to mildly interesting."

"You're many things." Pax looked at her, his dark eyes serious. "Boring isn't one of them."

Sage chewed her lip. "That's good to know." Unsure what else to say, she turned to watch the scenery pass by her window, relaxed into the soft leather seats, and listened to the low purr of the powerful engine.

Effectively settled into a peaceful little cocoon, she sighed when Pax pulled into a gravel parking lot between a single-story building painted a bright shade of blue and a playground full of equally colorful equipment.

"This is the local school we've been working with," Pax said as they climbed from the vehicle. "So far we've painted the entire exterior and interior of the building. We've installed all new playground equipment and added a soccer field. We start the landscaping in a few days. La Vida has funded everything. The staff, our guests, and parents at the school have donated all the labor."

"How do you pay for it?"

"Ten percent of La Vida's profits go to funding its social outreach program. Some of the inexpensive activities happen year round. The costly projects require more planning. We usually tackle one of those a month or even every other month if it's a particularly large project."

"I assume the projects at the school you just mentioned are the expensive ones. What other interactions are there?"

"We donate a lot of books to the local schools. Our guests read them to the kids to help their English. The kids, in turn, teach our guests words and phrases in Spanish."

Sage laughed. "I'm sure that can get interesting."

"Oh, yeah. After spending the day with a group of ten-year-old boys, one lady told Susanna her food was *wacala*. Apparently, the kids had told her it means delicious."

"What does it really mean?"

"Gross. Yuck. Disgusting."

Sage sucked in a breath. "That couldn't have ended well."

"Nope." Pax grinned. "Susanna threatened to feed the woman to a crocodile. Luckily, Brick calmed her down before she carried through with it."

"Never a dull moment, huh?"

His grin widened. "Never."

"You love them."

He shrugged. "They're family. Even if they drive you crazy, you've got to love them."

Sage's heart inflated like a balloon mortgage. Jeez-o-Pete. She liked him. She liked how he considered his staff family. And that he gave up a cushy, secure future to follow a dream. She liked that he'd built La Vida on the belief that people can give and receive in unison as long as they kept their hearts and minds open. She liked that he understood her. She liked that he didn't dismiss her fears, but he didn't let her hide from life because of them. And she liked that when he smiled at her, she wanted to make him smile right back.

Holy buckets. That was a lot of likes.

If she wasn't careful, she could fall for him—a totally stupid move since he didn't seem interested in catching her.

Sage needed to remember that Will was the sensible choice for her. She wouldn't have to change her life for him. With Will, she didn't have to risk making the same mistake her mother made again and again. And she lacked Pax's bravery. She could never risk a secure future to follow a dream.

She did a mental head shake and cleared her throat. "You mentioned landscaping?"

"It's what you'll be doing here in a few days."

"Not all of it, I hope."

He chuckled. "Don't worry. They'll be a lot of people helping out."

"Can I see the plans?"

"Yeah." He paused. "They're at my house. Why don't you come over for dinner tonight, and I'll show them to you."

"Oh. Okay. I guess that would be fine." Warning bells sounded in her head.

Dinner with Pax, alone, would be dangerous on many levels. She'd known for years that she couldn't trust her body to do the smart thing around him. Now, she feared she couldn't trust her heart either.

•••

Less than an hour later, Pax dropped Sage at the resort with instructions to head up the trail to his house whenever she was ready for dinner. She took a quick shower, brushed on light makeup, and paired an airy sundress with strappy sandals. As she left her villa and climbed the nearly hidden path from the beach to Pax's home, her heart pounded heavily in her chest. Maybe climbing the steep hill—rather than the excitement at spending the evening alone with Pax—had caused her rapid pulse?

"Yeah, right," she muttered, rolling her eyes at her own delusions.

She reached the end of the trail, stepped out of the thick canopy of foliage, and gasped at the sight of his home perched on a bluff overlooking the ocean.

From where she stood, she saw a beautiful outdoor living area nestled beside a serene infinity pool built along the edge of the bluff. The candlelit outdoor area had a natural stone floor, dark wood furniture topped with oversized neutral-colored cushions, open walls, and a steep roof supported by large wooden columns. It was lovely and peaceful, the epitome of Balinese-style perfection.

Pax emerged from the interior and moved toward her. Jeans and a black T-shirt hugged his frame. A devilish smile lit his eyes.

"I wasn't sure you would show. I'm grilling steaks and local vegetables, and I stole a loaf of Susanna's bread from La Vida's kitchen. If she finds out, she'll be ticked. Ever since the last pastry chef left, she's had to do all the baking, which isn't her strong suit. She won't even attempt to make the chocolate croissants we used to offer every morning. La Vida was known for them, although, I think I miss them more than the guests do." Pax gave a wry smile. "Can I get you something to drink?"

"Iced tea would be great." Sage hopped onto one of the bamboo barstools and made a sweeping gesture with her hand. "Your home is amazing."

"I designed and built as much of it myself as possible. Balinese style is starting to gain popularity in the area. I love how it invites nature inside by mixing indoor and outdoor spaces. But it incorporates a lot of hand-sculpted craftsmanship that's beyond my scope of abilities." Pax set a glass of tea in front of her and pulled steaks from the refrigerator. "So I hired local artisans to do the more intricate work."

Sage smiled. "It's good to know your limits."

His hands stilled and his dark eyes found hers. "I've always known my limits. But I've never been good at living within them."

"It seems you don't have to. Your family here consists of an Australian surfer, a Southern horseman, and a Latina firecracker. You drink Californian Cabernets with your dinner and eat chocolate croissants at breakfast. Your home is a Polynesian masterpiece in a Latin American paradise." She bit back a grin. "As far as I can tell, you have no limits."

"That's not true." He paused. "I can't have you."

Shocked, Sage sucked in a breath. "Do you want me?"

He quirked an eyebrow.

"I mean," she hurried to add, "do you want me for more than a night?"

"It doesn't matter."

"It matters to me." She hopped down from the stool to stand in front of Pax.

"We both know there is something between us." He gently tucked a loose strand of hair behind her ear. As if thinking better of the contact, he pulled back and shoved both of his hands into the front pockets of his jeans. "But if I asked you to stay, I don't think you would. And if you're not willing to give it a shot…" He shrugged. "Then what I want doesn't matter."

Sage felt her face drain of blood and her fingertips go numb. Had Pax just suggested she move to Costa Rica? Her mouth opened, but no words came out. She might be close to falling for him, but he hadn't said anything about love or commitment.

A painful vision of her childhood flashed through her mind. The spring of her sixth-grade year, her mother had moved them from Chicago to St. Louis to live with Clive Clumenaur, an artist she'd been dating for two whole weeks.

The transition had been incredibly hard for Sage. She'd missed her friends, her school, even their small apartment back in Chicago. By the winter, of course, her mom's relationship with the guy had ended in one final supernova blowup. So her mom moved them back to Chicago to hook up with the guy she'd dumped to move in with Clive in the first place.

A different version of the same story repeated three more times through junior high and high school. It had been a horrible way to live. The constant fear of being uprooted again, never having a true home. Sage couldn't do it again. She valued stability, and stability required commitment—not attraction, or lust, or whatever it was that Pax felt for her.

"Give it a shot?" She tipped her chin up and ignored the vise closing around her heart. "Are you suggesting I quit my job and move to Costa Rica so we can 'give it a shot?' What the hell does that even mean? We go on a few dates and reevaluate? What if you get sick of me in two weeks or two months or two years? Where does that leave me? In a foreign country. No boyfriend. No job. No home."

She clamped her mouth shut and glared at him. She took a deep breath and slowly blew it out. She needed to get control before she hyperventilated or cursed him out or pulled a total girl move and hurled one of his oversized throw pillows at his head.

Hands still in his pockets, Pax stared back at her with a resigned expression. "I understand."

His emotionless response drained her anger faster than she thought possible. Had she actually thought he'd profess his love and beg her to stay? If so, she was a bigger fool now than she'd been six years ago.

"Maybe I should leave?"

"My home or Costa Rica?" he asked in a tight voice.

"Both. I emailed my preliminary analysis of La Vida to Will yesterday. I can use the information I've gathered to prepare the final report from home."

Pax's jaw clenched and he nodded in silent acceptance.

Sage's heart squeezed even harder in her chest. She turned to leave before she did something really stupid like start crying.

"Sage, wait. I don't want—" Pax froze and his gaze flew to the door. His body went rigid. "What the hell?"

A knock on the front door triggered a hazy memory that dropped her stomach to her toes.

Before either of them could move, a lilting female voice drifted in the open windows on the warm ocean breeze.

"Paxton, dear, are you home?"

ELEVEN

UNBELIEVABLE. Talk about the worst freaking timing ever. Pax's stress level couldn't handle any more blasts from his past.

"He must be home. Katherine said that was his car." The familiar male voice sent another jolt of tension up his spine.

Damn. It was worse than he thought.

He leaned close to Sage since his open windows left nothing in the way of privacy. "This isn't over," he whispered. "Don't leave Costa Rica. Not yet."

Chewing on her lower lip, Sage nodded, and then her gaze darted from the front door to the trail leading away from his house.

"Don't even think about it," he warned. "No way am I facing them alone."

"Try to be patient. They really do love you."

"Huh. I just don't get why they're here," he mumbled more to himself than to her.

Sage made a strangled sound beside him.

He dropped his gaze to her. "What?"

"There's a chance that I kind of, maybe, sort of invited them to visit."

"You're kidding me. When?" he demanded stepping toward her.

She shuffled backwards, cringing. "Last night. From your phone. I may have sent an email inviting them."

"May have?"

"Okay. I did," she admitted in a rush.

"You sent it from my phone. Do they think it was from me?" His voice shot up a notch.

"Maybe. I signed your name on the email." She stepped around the couch in an obvious attempt to put space and furniture between them. "In my defense, I was a little tipsy when I sent it, and I didn't think they would get here until I'd already left."

"That wouldn't make it any better," he roared.

She shrugged. "It would have for me. I think it's best if you spend some quality alone time with your parents. I'll see you later."

Before he could stop her, Sage sped through his backyard and down the trail leading to the resort.

Unbelievable. First Kat and now this. He really would kill Sage this time. He rubbed a rough hand through his hair and counted to ten. Then he counted to ten again and grudgingly walked to the front door at the sound of a more demanding second knock.

Pax swung the door open. His smiling mother and stone-faced father stood directly in front of him with large suitcases at their sides.

"Oh, Paxton! It's so good to see you!" His mom rushed at him, wrapping her arms around his waist in a much stronger embrace than you would expect from such a slender woman. Then again, no one had ever called Ann Bennett weak. "We are so glad you finally invited us to visit. I hope it's okay that we came so quickly. We just couldn't wait any longer to see it for ourselves."

She released him but only took a small step away. "Isn't that right, Richard?" she asked in a tone that brooked no argument.

Pax looked at his dad. Richard Bennett had always been a big man, his presence commanding attention. But now, even though it had only been a few years since he last saw him, Richard's hair looked grayer than black, and his face had thinned with age. He appeared healthy, just not quite as large as he used to seem.

His dad cleared his throat. "Yes, I wanted to see what made this place so damn special." Under his breath he added, "It must be great since you gave up everything for it."

And here we go again.

"Richard, we're here to support Paxton's dreams, not to create problems for him. Remember that, or I'll call the jet to take you home immediately."

Pax raised an eyebrow. "You have a jet now?"

"Oh no, no. Owning a private jet alone is very expensive." His mom leaned around him to peek inside. "We share it with three other families. We have to juggle our schedule around theirs."

"Hmm. Sounds rough." Pax tried to keep a straight face.

His mom swatted his arm playfully. "I know full well how privileged we are to have this lifestyle. But don't forget, I grew up on a farm. I learned about hard work and sacrifice at an early age. You never forget those lessons." With that, his mom stepped past him to walk fully into his home and, up until that moment, his sanctuary. "Don't mind me, I'm going to show myself around."

"You get it from her, you know?" His dad shuffled uncomfortably. "Still beats the hell out of me why you choose to do things the hard way." He bent down and picked up his suitcase before following his wife into Pax's home.

Half in shock, Pax remained immobile at his front door as his parents wandered around his living room and backyard. First Sage, then Kat, and now his parents. How had all the disappointment and heartache he'd left in Silver Bay found him here?

His mom stepped back into the house from the outdoor living area. "There are two glasses on the counter. Are you entertaining?"

Only the thought of running away. "No."

"You would get more afternoon sun on the pool if you put it on the other side of your yard," his dad yelled from the backyard. "Ever thought about moving it?"

Pax grimaced and raked a hand through his hair. "No."

"Dear, can you show me where your guest room is? I'd like to unpack and freshen up before dinner. Kat invited us to the hacienda tonight, and Sage is here too. It will be just like old times! Won't that be fun?"

No. Pax gritted his teeth, stepped from his front door, and led the way to his guest room.

Family could be such a pain in the ass.

•••

Sage slipped from bed before sunrise and tiptoed to the bathroom, hoping not to disturb Kat. Halfway through her shower, she realized she hadn't scanned her bathroom for unwanted reptilian visitors when she first entered. Hmm. The jungle bathroom must be growing on her...

When she crept from the villa thirty minutes later, soft dawn light filtered through the trees and the boisterous calls of the native birds greeted her. She grinned, enjoying the warm breeze that rustled the leaves and swished her hair about her shoulders as she followed the path to the hacienda.

When she reached the hacienda, sounds of activity and the smell of fresh bread drifted from the kitchen. She took a deep breath, tipped her chin up, and pulled her shoulders back. She couldn't show any fear if her plan was going to work.

Sage stepped into the kitchen, which gleamed with natural stone countertops and high-end stainless steel appliances. She scanned the room until her gaze landed on the chef. Susanna was furiously chopping peppers and barking orders in Spanish at the same time. Though Sage cringed inwardly at the knife in the chef's hand, she couldn't back down now.

"*Buenos días*, Susanna. I'd like your permission to make chocolate croissants for the guests."

Susanna lifted her eyes from the dish she'd been preparing and wiped her hands on her apron. Without saying a word, she stared at Sage with an intensity that made her gut clench. Sage held the other woman's gaze and bit down on the inside of her bottom lip. She couldn't lose this stare down.

After what felt like an hour, but was likely less than a minute, Susanna gave a full-bodied sigh. Then she dipped her head as if granting her royal approval and pointed to an open work space.

"*Gracias.*" Sage hurried to get started before the almighty ruler of the kitchen changed her regal mind.

Sage gathered the supplies and the recipe card for the chocolate croissants. She knew croissants were difficult to make and that many amateur and even some experienced bakers refused to attempt them. Luckily, she had an innate talent for baking, and while the recipe looked complicated and would take a lot of time to make, it seemed doable.

She'd always found peace in the kitchen and today was no exception. With her hands in dough, her mind wandered to the previous evening.

After the near silent treatment that the Bennett boys had pulled at dinner last night, Sage had serious doubts about her reckless invitation. Neither son nor dad said more than "pass the wine" the entire time. Once the brief, awkward dinner had finished, everyone had looked pretty relieved to go their separate ways for the rest of the evening.

Sage knew how difficult and unsupportive Richard had always been about Pax's dream of building La Vida. She also knew Richard hadn't asked for, and might not even deserve, a second chance, but she still hoped Pax would give him one.

After the painful dinner, she had decided to try her hand at making the chocolate croissants Pax mentioned loving so much. She figured she owed him that much since she'd sent a falsified invitation to his borderline estranged parents and all.

"Are you doing it right?"

Sage jumped at the sound of Susanna's voice behind her.

"I think so. I'm about to put the dough in the refrigerator. I'll clean up here and be back to work on the next step of the recipe when it's chilled."

Susanna nodded. "This looks good. Maybe better than mine. You can make them tomorrow too," she added as she walked away.

Sage smiled to herself, confident this was Susanna's version of lavish praise.

"She likes you."

She looked up. Pax stood leaning against the arched doorway with his arms crossed over his chest.

"I'm winning her over one baked good at a time." She finished wrapping the dough and placed it in the industrial-sized refrigerator. "How are you doing this morning?"

Pax groaned, dipped his head, and rubbed the back of his neck with his hand. "I keep thinking karma's done with me, but then she gets one more kick in when I'm not looking."

"Your dad being a pain?"

"For the most part, he's silent and scowling. So Mom is filling the silence with constant chatter about things I never needed or wanted to know." Pax began to pace the kitchen. "She told me all about the knee pain Dr. Cambridge, Silver Bay's longtime veterinarian, has been dealing with. She also told me my sisters started puberty late so she thinks that's why they look so young for their age."

Sage grinned.

"It's not funny," Pax grumbled, his brow furrowed. "No matter how hard I try, I'll never be able to forget that information."

"How long are they staying?"

He locked his gaze on hers, suddenly serious. "They leave in two days."

The same day she left.

"Why did you do it?" he asked.

She didn't bother pretending to not understand his question. "Because La Vida is special. What you're doing here, with the community and with your guests, is really great. You deserve to keep her."

"My loan—"

"Won't get approved," Sage interrupted gently. "Without a larger down payment, there's a good chance Pembrock will deny your application."

"Is that why you brought them here?" Pax's voice rose in anger. "You want me to ask Mommy and Daddy for money? Damn it, Sage, I thought you knew me better than that."

"You spend your time trying to show people that it's good to both give and receive help." Sage stepped toward him, her voice also rising in frustration. "Doesn't that apply to you? Are you too good to get help from people who love you? Jeez-o-Pete, Pax, we all need help sometimes."

"Not from him." Pax shoved his fisted hands into his pockets and shook his head. "He doesn't want to help me."

"And I didn't want to come to Costa Rica or ride a horse through the jungle or shower in a bathroom wide-open to slimy reptiles or learn to surf, but I did all those things. And guess what?" She paused, shaking her head in wonder as a grin tugged at her lips. "I'm happy I did."

Pax sighed. "I've fought with him for years. He won't change his mind."

"You don't know that. Show him La Vida. Give him a chance."

"I'll try." Pax dropped his head and rubbed the back of his neck again. "But we might kill each other if we have to live together for the next two days."

"You're a creative, resourceful, intelligent man. I'm sure you can find a way to get space from your parents."

His head shot up and a devilish gleam lit his eyes. "You're right. I run a resort after all." With palpable excitement, Pax spun on his heel. "I'll catch you in a bit," he said over his shoulder and charged from the room.

"Oh boy," Sage murmured to herself. She really hoped his excitement didn't involve evicting her and Kat from their villa so his parents could stay there instead. Sure, she probably deserved it after interfering with his life the way she had. She chewed her lip. Hopefully, his generous nature would beat back any thoughts of revenge he might be harboring.

She finished cleaning her work area, slipped the apron from around her neck, and hung it on one of the hooks mounted along the wall. In the main room, she spotted Brick at the coffee bar. He stood with a cup in his hand, staring toward the outdoor tables with a frown settled between his eyes.

She joined him at the bar and began filling her own cup of steaming, fragrant coffee from the thermos. "Something wrong?" she asked him.

Brick shifted his eyes to her. "Oh, hi, little lady. Didn't see you there." He took a drink of his coffee and looked back to the area he'd been staring at before. "I'm wondering why Pax is kicking that couple out of La Vida."

"What?" Sage followed Brick's line of sight and saw Pax deep in conversation with the older couple she'd seen around the resort all week. "What's he doing?"

"He's asking them to move to a different hotel for the rest of the week. He's never done anything like this before. He must be real desperate to free up their villa. He would have to be to risk an annual."

"An annual?"

"Yes, ma'am. That's what we call the guests who come back every year."

Holy buckets. Sage fiddled with the necklace she'd slipped on that morning as Mr. and Mrs. Floral Print and Pax rose from the table and shook hands. Thankfully, no one appeared angry or offended. In fact, they all seemed quite happy if their smiling faces were to be believed.

As the couple moved down the path toward the villas, Pax headed directly toward her, a look of triumph written in big, bold print across his handsome face.

He stopped directly in front of her but looked at Brick. "Can you drive the Kiplingers to their new hotel? They're leaving shortly."

"Sure, boss." Brick set his coffee on the bar and took off in the same direction the couple had just headed.

Pax turned to her with a satisfied expression. "The Kiplingers are going to finish the rest of their stay at a five-star resort not far from here. My parents can move to their villa after we return from zip-lining this afternoon."

Sage bit the inside of her lip and shifted her weight from one flip-flopped foot to the other. "How did you manage that?"

"I called in a favor."

"Are your parents going to be okay moving?"

Pax blew out a breath, leaned forward to rest his forearms against the bar, and began drumming the fingers of his right hand on the dark wood surface. "Mom will like being closer to the beach. And Dad will like being farther from me. It's a win-win," he muttered.

Sage sighed, set her coffee down, and gently laid both of her hands over his. "Pax..." She paused, waiting until his fingers stilled beneath hers. "He loves you. But he doesn't understand the choices you've made. Now's the perfect chance to make him understand. The fact that he's even here means he's willing to try."

"Uh-huh," he replied, one eyebrow raised.

"That's the spirit," she said, ignoring the skepticism radiating from every cell of his body.

He shrugged. "It's not like things can get much worse."

"Oh jeez, don't say that. You're going to jinx it. Things can always get—"

"Hello, Sage."

Sage gasped, yanked her hands back, and spun around at the sound of the familiar voice behind her.

"Will?" she stammered.

She'd tried to warn Pax. Things could always get worse.

TWELVE

"WHAT are you doing here?" Sage took a deep breath to control the squeak in her voice and tried again. "I mean, I didn't realize you were coming." She moved toward her boss—or was it boyfriend?—and away from Pax, turning on her highest watt smile.

"After I read your analysis, I wanted to see this place for myself." Will scanned the room, his gaze stopping on Pax. "So quaint."

The men stared at each other in silence before Pax extended his right hand. "Good to see you again, Will."

Will scanned the room as he slowly reached his hand out to shake Pax's. "I have to admit, I was surprised by Sage's glowing report. I never thought she'd enjoy a resort specializing in adventure."

"This place offers its guests a lot more than adventure," Sage said. "Once you spend a couple of days here, I'm sure you'll appreciate the natural beauty and tranquil atmosphere La Vida exudes."

AMELIA JUDD

As if on cue, ear-splitting shrieks, howls, and grunts filled the air around them. The sounds hit roughly the same decibel level as a heavy metal concert. Sage saw, and very much heard, two ticked-off monkeys in a heated shouting match in the trees surrounding the pool deck.

"What is all that ruckus?" Will took a step back and scanned the trees with a horrified look on his face.

"Don't worry, folks," Brick yelled over the noise as he stepped onto the pool deck. "That's probably two boy monkeys fighting over who gets the gal monkey. But I do reckon it's best we all step back before they start flinging poop."

"Does this sort of thing happen often?" Will retreated further into the hacienda as the other guests scrambled for cover around them.

"It's never happened before," Pax said with a pained expression. "This week is full of surprises," he added under his breath.

"You're in luck, Will," Sage said, plastering on a smile and yelling over the howling monkeys. "There are hardly any vacancies here, but a villa just became available." She turned her gaze to Pax. "Rather than moving the other guests into the open villa, I suggest Will stay there instead. Being on property is the only way for him to truly experience all of La Vida."

Pax drew in a long, slow breath as if bracing himself for the inevitable. Then he nodded his consent.

"Excellent." Will placed his hand on the small of her back and leaned close to be heard. "Why don't you show me around the resort? Let's start in the opposite direction of those wild animals."

120

Fighting the urge to step away, Sage watched Pax's gaze drop to Will's hand at her waist and then return to her eyes. Jeez. If Pax ground his jaw any harder, his teeth might turn to dust.

"Pax should show you around. He knows the resort better than anyone," she suggested.

"Nonsense. I'm sure he has guests to attend to, and to be honest, I also traveled here so we could spend some time together outside of the office. Costa Rica sounded so romantic." He frowned. "It goes without saying that I didn't know flying fecal matter would be an issue."

"There's nothing to worry about." Sage gestured toward the trees. "See, the monkeys have quieted down already. I'm sure no one is going to get hit by poop today."

Pax cocked an eyebrow.

"Not literally, at least," she muttered under her breath.

She gulped, and her gaze darted between the two men. Daggers shot from Pax's eyes as his hands clenched and unclenched at his side. Will fidgeted with his watch, looking out of place and uneasy.

Things could get really ugly, really fast if she didn't navigate the next few days carefully. So much for choosing the banking industry as a secure foundation for building a stable future. At this rate, her life would have been more stable, and less nerve-racking, if she'd pursued a career as a circus tightrope walker.

•••

As Will left with Sage, Pax gritted his teeth and swallowed down the urge to yank the guy off of her. She didn't need a knight in shining armor. She'd always been strong, capable, and completely upfront about the fact that she would never walk away from a stable future to be with him.

It didn't matter how much he enjoyed spending time with her. And it absolutely didn't matter how much he wanted her to stay.

"How long have you been in love with her?" Kat asked. She stood a few feet away, head tipped to the side, a knowing expression on her face.

"What the hell are you talking about? Did your surfboard hit you on the head?" He strode out of the main room and headed for his office.

Of course, his sister followed him there.

"I'm talking about Sage." Kat closed the door. "I can't believe I never realized it before. You're gaga over her."

"I am not gaga over her."

She grinned. "If you could have seen what was written all over your face a minute ago, you wouldn't have the balls to deny it."

"I'm not talking about this with you." Pax paced in front of his desk and dragged a hand through his hair.

"You need to talk to someone about it. Might as well be me."

"No way. Time for you to—" Pax stopped mid-sentence.

His father's laughter drifted through the closed door. Until that moment, he hadn't realized how long it had been since he'd heard his old man laugh.

Curious to see what he sounded so happy about, Pax stepped into the main room in time to see Richard clamp his hand onto Will's shoulder as the two men vigorously shook hands.

Terrific. His dad was looking at Will like he was the educated, polished, professional son he'd always wanted. Not only did it burn that his father preferred Will to him, it pissed him off that his old man couldn't see Claire was a better fit for Bennett Industries than Pax would ever be.

His oldest sister was a hard worker, smart as hell, and capable of accomplishing anything she set her mind to. Claire had even told him the last time they spoke on the phone that she actually enjoyed working with their dad and didn't mind being stuck in an office all day. Pax couldn't think of a worse frigging way to spend a day, let alone a lifetime.

"Buck up. Dad only likes him because he kisses his ass," Kat whispered, digging her fingers into his arm and pulling him toward the group.

While a few guests had returned to the tables inside the hacienda and on the patio surrounding the pool, the main commotion came from the center of the open-aired room where his mom, dad, and Will were enthusiastically greeting each other.

Positioned a few feet from the group, Sage toyed with her silver necklace. Her eyes darted nervously between Pax, his father, and Will.

"Pax, why didn't you tell me this son of a bitch was going to be here?" His dad's voice boomed as he slapped Will on the shoulder.

Pax smiled in a half-assed attempt to mimic Richard's joking demeanor. "Because I didn't know the son of a bitch was going to be here."

Sage sucked in air and Kat squeezed his arm in warning.

"I invited him to zip-line with us today," his old man added, oblivious to the tension. "I tried to get Sage to join us too, but she keeps telling me no. Maybe you can get a yes out of her."

Pax raised an eyebrow and turned to Sage in silent inquiry.

"Nope." She shook her head vehemently back and forth. "I've got work to do in the kitchen. I'm close to winning Susanna over. I can't desert her now to go swinging through the trees."

"You can bake when we get back," Kat said. "Please, come with us."

"Yes, dear, we'd all like you to join us," Pax's mom added with a smile.

"Sage isn't the type to enjoy zip-lining." Will sidled up to Sage and wrapped an arm around her waist. "I'll stay with her."

"Thank you for the offer, Will, but I'll be fine here alone."

"I insist," Will said.

A knot tightened in Pax's chest. He should be fighting to get his loan approved, but instead he had to hang out with his stress-inducing family while the woman he couldn't get out of his mind spent a romantic day with another guy at his freaking resort.

•••

Less than two hours later, Sage's stomach dropped to her expensive, new hiking boots as she peeked over the edge of a frighteningly deep canyon. What the heck had she been thinking? Right now, she could be safely back at the hacienda baking decadent sweets. But no, Pax had looked so darn disappointed when she'd turned down his offer, she'd changed her stupid mind about going zip-lining. Now, standing on the rim of a four-hundred-foot drop and rigged up in an intimidating number of safety straps and a battered red helmet, rational thought returned with a vengeance.

"Regretting your decision to join us?" Pax asked, stepping next to her.

"Immensely."

"You're going to love it."

She shot him a look of incredulous disbelief. "Have you met me?" she asked, her voice rising in panic. "And why is my helmet all beat up? What the heck happened to the last person who wore it? Seriously? Did they run into a tree?"

He grinned down at her. "There are double cables and double pulleys. It's completely safe. The course starts at the top of the canyon and then travels back and forth across it until we reach the bottom. There are a dozen runs in all. The longest is over a third of a mile long."

"What if I hate the first one so much, I don't want to do the rest of them?"

"If that happens, you can ride tandem with me for the rest of the day."

Sage sucked in a breath. "That might be awkward with your parents here," she said, looking to see if the others were watching their conversation.

Thankfully, Kat and Pax's parents stood next to Brick, their attention completely focused on the older guide. Making large swooping motions with his hands, Brick looked to be in the middle of another one of his animated stories.

"Not as awkward as it would be with your boyfriend here," Pax added dryly.

She turned her attention to Will, who was standing a few feet from Richard. Staring at her with a sour expression on his face, he looked weighed down with all the gear wrapped around his thin frame. And he looked ticked.

Sage smiled weakly at him and turned back to Pax. "He's not my boyfriend," she hissed.

"Does he know that?"

"Of course. We've only been out a few times."

"Uh-huh."

Sage cocked her head. "Do you think I'm lying?"

"No." His expression hardened. "I think he takes a few dates more seriously than you do."

She glanced at Will. His jaw was clenched, his features were tense, and he looked even more ticked now than he had a minute ago. Worry churned her belly. Will was a decent guy, and she didn't want to hurt him. If she lived through zip-lining, she'd have to find a way to let him down easy. Being around Pax again had finally made her realize she needed to be with a man who reached all the way to her heart.

"Brick's about to give directions." Pax's voice broke into her thoughts. "I'm sure you'll want to hear this."

"Absolutely." Sage hurried to join the others before she could miss any important piece of safety information.

"Hiya, folks." Brick smiled widely at the group. "Before we get started, there's just one rule I want you to remember. Always keep your gloved hand behind you and wrapped around the cable. Squeeze the cable with that hand to stop."

Eyes wide, Sage raised her hand.

"Yes, ma'am."

"What if we let go of the cable by mistake?"

"You'll start spinning faster than a tornado in a trailer park."

Holy buckets. That sounded bad. Sage raised her hand again.

"Yes, little lady."

"What should we do if we accidentally let go?"

He shook his head. "Just don't let go."

Eyebrows to her hairline, she shot her hand up again.

"You'll be fine," Pax murmured in her ear as he gently lowered her arm. "You'll see a lot of monkeys, parrots, and a beautiful river once we reach the bottom of the canyon. You're going to love it."

"So you keep telling me," she grumbled, trying to ignore his touch and the warm tickle of his breath along her temple.

She felt him smile next to her and her body perked up in interest. Maybe she should reconsider riding tandem with him? Being strapped tightly to Pax might actually make the whole experience enjoyable. Jeez, she had to get control of the weird combination of fear, adrenaline, and arousal coursing through her before she made a fool of herself.

Petrified, Sage watched first Brick and then Logan hook onto the line and soar through the air to the second platform. Pax hooked Kat up next. Her best friend happily jumped off the edge as if gliding four hundred feet over a canyon was no big deal. Ann screamed in joy on her turn, and Richard and Will shouted in excitement during their respective flights. Soon, only Sage and Pax remained on the platform.

"Ready?" he asked her.

She shook her head.

"Do you want to ride with me?"

She blew out a sigh. "Yes. For all the wrong reasons."

He grinned.

"Any chance I can talk you out of this?"

His grin turned wicked. "I'm sure you could persuade me."

"Really?" she asked hopefully.

"Honey, you could get me to do about anything. But if you walk away now, you'll always regret it. Don't let fear control you." He held out his hand to her. "I know you, Sage. And I promise you, you're going to love it."

"Fine." She rolled her eyes and put her hand in his. "But if I fall to my death, I'm going to curse your name the entire way down."

"Fair enough." Pax tugged her gently to his side and began fastening her to the line. He tested the buckles and reminded her where to hold on. Then he moved behind her and wrapped his hands around her hips. "I'm going to help you push off."

"What? Why?"

"You're pretty light so there's a chance you could stop before you get to the end if you don't have enough momentum."

"You're just now telling me this!" Her mouth went dry, and her pulse pounded in her throat.

"Relax. If it happens, spin around and use your hands to pull yourself along the line until you get to the end. Easy. Safe travels," he said as he pushed her off the edge.

Before she could put coherent words together, Sage was zipping over the jungle canopy at a blinding speed. Resisting the urge to close her eyes and scream, she craned her head in every direction, taking in the blue sky above her and the winding river way, way, way below her. Unbelievably, rather than scared, she felt... amazing.

For once in her life, she felt brave and adventurous and exciting. As the lush, green forest on the far side of the canyon grew closer, she didn't want the ride to end. Pax had been right. She loved zip-lining!

Sage slowed to a stop a few feet from where the line ended on the far side of the canyon. She smiled widely as Brick unfastened her from the line and secured her to the platform. "That was awesome!"

"Glad you liked it 'cause we've got eleven more to go."

Suddenly, eleven didn't seem like nearly enough. Sage wanted to spend the entire day flying through the trees. No one, except Pax, would ever believe that she—safe, responsible, boring Sage—had turned into an adrenaline junkie!

THIRTEEN

AFTER her exhilarating morning, Sage spent a peaceful afternoon in La Vida's kitchen. By early evening, she was pulling her first batch of chocolate croissants from the oven. She held the baking sheet close to her nose, closed her eyes, and inhaled the warm, buttery scent of heaven on earth. If her golden morsels of perfection tasted even a fraction as good as they smelled, Pax would love them.

When she looked through the front window and spotted him talking to a groundskeeper, Sage dropped a couple of croissants into a pastry bag and hurried out the side exit.

"Pax…" She paused until he looked her way, a tired smile pulling at the corners of his mouth. "Do you have time for a walk?" She held up the bag of pastries for him to see. "I brought goodies."

"Bribery?"

"Yep."

"Unneeded." He took her hand. "Come on, there's a private path down to a stretch of beach the guests don't know about." He directed her to a narrow dirt trail leading into the trees along the kitchen side of the hacienda. "We won't be able to stay long. I've got to meet your boss to go over some financial reports before dinner."

She squeezed his hand in support, appreciating the calluses that roughened his palm. Pax gave everything he had—physically, mentally, emotionally—to make La Vida a success.

Her own dedication paled in comparison. Sure, she worked hard. But she did so from fear of losing her job, not because she held any real passion for it. If she won the lottery tomorrow, she would quit the second the check cleared. If Pax came into unexpected millions, he would never walk away from La Vida—he would pour even more into it.

At the end of the winding trail, they stepped through an opening in the trees onto a small stretch of sand. A few large boulders jutted into the water, making a natural division with the main beach the guests used.

Pax led her to the shade of a palm tree and sank down to recline in the sand, bracing his elbows behind him. Sitting down next to him, Sage reached into the pastry bag, pulled a warm croissant out, and offered it to him. "I made these for you. They took a long time, so I would appreciate if you pretend to like them no matter how they taste."

His eyes lit up. "Chocolate croissants." He took a big bite. "You're a godsend," he said, groaning in appreciation.

"Glad you like them. Susanna said I could make them again tomorrow. Actually, I'm pretty sure she ordered me to make them tomorrow." Sage grinned and sucked a chocolate covered finger into her mouth.

Pax groaned again.

She looked up to find his gaze locked on the finger in her mouth. She froze.

"Could you please stop doing that?" he asked in a strained voice.

"Sorry, but my fingers are a mess, and I don't want to get chocolate all over my clothes. Look the other away if it bothers you."

"I have a better idea." Pax snatched her wrist, pulled her hand to his mouth, and wrapped his warm, wet lips around one of her fingers. Slowly, seductively he licked off every ounce of chocolate.

She heard a soft moan from somewhere close by. When Pax's eyes snapped to her parted lips, she realized the sound must have come from her. She should probably be embarrassed, but as long as no drool actually came out of her mouth, she was proud to be holding it relatively together in the face of such temptation.

Pax dropped her wrist and fell back to lie in the sand. "Sorry. I don't have much control around you."

"I know the feeling," she muttered to herself and fisted her hands in her lap.

"So you're meeting with Will?" she asked, hoping to change the subject and clear the R-rated thoughts from her mind.

"Yep. He said we needed to discuss the issues with my loan in private."

"Ouch."

"That didn't sound good to me either." Pax exhaled a long breath. "Nothing is definite, though, so there's still a chance the bank will give me the money." Pax stood up and offered her his hand. "I've got to head back to meet with him."

Sage shook her head gently and rose without taking his hand. "Nothing personal, but it's best if we don't touch."

"Afraid you won't be able to resist me?" Pax asked, his gaze holding hers.

"No," she lied.

He cocked an eyebrow and stared her down.

"Fine! Yes. I'm afraid I won't be able to resist you," she snapped. "Satisfied?"

Pax gave a mirthless chuckle. "Honey, I'm not even close to satisfied."

•••

Less than a half hour later, Pax watched Will pace his office and wondered what the hell Sage saw in this tool. She needed someone who challenged her, not a kiss-ass, yes-man that Pax had determined Will to be after meeting him at one of Ann Bennett's famous charity events years ago.

"You need to understand," Will said. "You've put my bank in a very uncomfortable position by requesting this loan. Usually we wouldn't consider a loan going to an international location, but your father's business is very important to us. We don't want to jeopardize our relationship with him by denying your loan."

"Okay. Then approve it," Pax said dryly.

Will snorted. "You're not even close to having the down payment we normally require for a loan of this magnitude."

"Can't you lower that number based on La Vida's history of financial growth and stability?" Pax gestured to the papers on the desk in front of him. "If you look at her financial records, you'll see how successful she is."

Will waved away his offer. "That won't be necessary. I studied all of those documents before I traveled here. Though the resort's numbers are impressive, the fact remains that you will have very little of your own money invested in the venture. If you get tired of running La Vida and decide to walk away, my bank will end up owning a resort in a foreign market where we have no area of knowledge."

"I won't walk away from her."

"Your history suggests otherwise. You quit college, deserted Bennett Industries, and have cut off nearly all ties with your family and your hometown. When it comes to the future, you're not a good bet."

"Get to your point, Pembrock," Pax growled.

"My point is that when I return to Milwaukee, I will discuss your loan with my father. But you should know, unless there is a significant change in the circumstances, your loan will likely not be approved."

FOURTEEN

SAGE patted down the dirt around the small green bush she'd just planted at the playground, sat back on her heels, and swiped the sweat from her forehead.

"You make a great landscaper. Remind me to double your pay."

She looked up to see Pax examining the work she'd completed so far. "I thought my pay was the satisfaction of a job well done?" She squinted to protect her eyes from the glare of the afternoon sun.

"Yep. Consider it doubled." A faint smile pulled at the corners of his mouth. "Do you need help finishing your area?"

She wrinkled her nose and shook her head. "I'm covered with bug repellent, sunblock, sweat, and dirt. Trust me, no one wants to get close to me right now. Besides, everyone looks pretty busy."

She scanned the yard of the local school. She'd been working there alongside a group of thirty or so volunteers for the past three hours. They'd accomplished a lot so far, removing debris and brush, pulling weeds, and clearing away overgrown bushes. The teams of workers were now planting tons of flowers and small bushes in order to create a landscaped perimeter around the small playground and soccer field next to the school building.

While Kat, Richard, and Ann worked with a large group clearing away a brushy area near the back of the property, Sage had been assigned the job of landscaping a semicircular flowerbed along the side of the school. An assortment of bushes, greenery, and colorful flowers in pots sat next to the area, waiting for her to place and plant them all.

She loved the gratifying results of seeing the flowerbed she designed in her mind take physical shape before her. It reminded her of the sense of fulfillment she felt creating in the kitchen. Too bad analyzing loan requests didn't provide her the same satisfaction.

Maybe she should have followed Pax's example. He'd chosen a riskier but also more rewarding path in life. She'd chosen the safe path, the smart path. An unmistakable twinge of regret squeezed her heart. What if she'd chosen wrong?

"You're doing a good thing here." Sage looked again at Pax. "La Vida, the school, the community, Costa Rica, all of it. You should be proud."

"Thanks," he said, not meeting her gaze. "But it's not just me." He gestured around the schoolyard. "We could never complete these projects without La Vida's staff, guests, and local families volunteering as well."

"I saw you greet everyone by name with a handshake and a smile. How do you know them all?" she asked.

"La Vida has funded projects for the school before. Last year, I worked with many of them when we painted it."

"They like you. Which is no surprise. Watching you work is like watching a documentary on exceptional leadership."

He raised a skeptical eyebrow.

"I mean it. You're a great leader. You're not bossy. You give clear directions on what needs to be done, but you're not a demanding control freak on how to get to the end results." Sage reached for her water bottle and took a long gulp.

Pax rubbed the back of his neck and shook his head. "You're giving me too much credit."

"Not at all. You're patient with questions, you work hard, and you're willing to help out wherever you're needed." She stood up and gestured to the group of people working around them. "Most importantly, you're nice to everyone, even when things aren't going well. I know some people see it as a weakness, but it takes a lot more strength to show kindness in difficult situations than it does to be a jerk."

"Kindness is one of the few things I can afford," Pax muttered.

"I'm glad your dad came along today," she said carefully.

"Yeah, I thought he was going to golf with Will," he said with a shrug, "but he texted this morning. Said he decided to help at the school instead."

She laid her hand on his arm. "He likes it here."

He closed his eyes and inhaled deeply. A moment later, his expression hardened, and he stepped out of her reach. "Unlikely."

He turned to watch Brick and Logan lug a heavy-looking bench toward the playground. They grunted with exertion as they passed.

"We're fine. No need to lend a hand, ay," Logan called to them. "Thanks anyway for your numerous offers of help."

"Your accent makes it hard for me to tell if you're being sarcastic or not," Sage responded, widening her eyes in mock innocence. "Plus, think how big your muscles will be after today's work."

A devilish smile lit Logan's eyes. "You like my muscles, darl? Once I set this bench down, I'll come over and flex for you."

A low growl rumbled from Pax's throat.

Sage chuckled. "He's harmless."

"So you keep telling me."

"Damn, big brother, you sound like a pouty chick," Kat said as she and Ann walked up to them.

Pax didn't answer her, but he did give her the same exasperated look that Kat's bluntness triggered in many people.

"Don't tell me you're jealous of that meathead." A few pieces of loose dirt flew off of Kat's gloved hand as she gestured toward Logan. "You're built like an Olympic swimmer. Thor over there is too bulky. Women don't dig that."

Sage fought back a grin and glanced at Ann. The older woman had an intrigued, almost shrewd look in her eye as she observed the conversation between two of her children.

"Great. I'm Flipper and he's the God of Thunder," Pax grumbled.

Kat snorted. "He's goddamn annoying, that's what he is."

Ann cleared her throat. "Katherine, I know you like to use vulgarities to express yourself, but please remember that Logan is Paxton's friend." Ann patted Pax's arm. "I think your friend is very nice, and for what it's worth, dear, I think you two are both very handsome young men."

Pax groaned and dropped his head. "Did you two need something?"

"Nope," Kat slugged his shoulder. "Mom and I were just taking a little break and thought we'd see what you two were chit-chatting about. Looked like the convo was getting hot and—"

"It's time Katherine and I get back to work," Ann said, cutting off Kat's words. "That brush isn't going to clear itself." Ann looped her arm in Kat's and gracefully led her away.

Pax blew out a breath. "I still can't believe you invited them here."

Sage grinned. "At least today you sound more resigned than angry by the fact. That's progress," she added in an overly cheery voice.

He cocked an eyebrow, but before he could respond, a dark-haired little girl ran up, grabbed one of his hands with both of hers, and leaned all her weight backward in a futile attempt to budge his large frame. The girl's pants had a few grass stains from working outside, and her pretty face was smudged with dirt.

After digging for hours, Sage's designer adventure clothes were covered in similar stains, and her face likely sported a few matching smudges of yuck.

"Mr. Paxton, Mamá said to get you. She needs you to help."

"*Está bien*, Celia. *No te preoccupies*," Pax said. "Celia, this is Sage. Can you stay and help her plant the rest of the bushes if I go help your mamá?

Celia eyed Sage with ocean-sized waves of skepticism pouring from her big brown eyes. After a long moment of consideration, she gave Pax a cautious nod of agreement.

"Great." He knelt down to the little girl's eye level. "Sage is a very nice lady, but she isn't used to working outside. She needs a helper with strong muscles to get everything planted by the end of the day."

Celia nodded her understanding and turned back to Sage with a look resembling pity on her solemn little face as Pax strode away.

"Hi, Celia," Sage said with a smile. "I'm glad you're here to help me. We have all of those bushes and flowers left to plant." She gestured to her right where the plants waited to find a home. "Can you help me decide where everything should go?"

Celia's eyes widened and a tentative smile pulled at her lips. She hurried over to study the remaining plants and carefully selected one with a few large leaves branching off from a thick green stalk.

"Nice choice," Sage said. "Where should we put it?"

The little girl studied the flowerbed, walking through it multiple times before pointing to a position of importance near the front of the design.

Sage went to work digging a hole and transferring the plant to its new home while Celia picked what they should plant next.

They continued the teamwork for the next hour. Celia designing and Sage planting. The language barrier meant they didn't talk much, but they shared a lot of smiles and a few giggles. Celia chose a spot for their final plant in the far back corner of the flowerbed where two large rocks were stacked together.

The rocks didn't look too heavy, so Sage gripped the top rock and braced her feet.

Celia pointed toward the space between the two rocks. "*Serpient,*" she calmly announced.

Sage's breath caught in her throat as her heart dropped to her feet. Oh. Holy. Buckets. Her hands were inches from a snake!

Fighting the instinct to run like hell, she slowly pulled her hands away from the rock. She stepped in front of Celia and locked her eyes on the rounded, speckled head of a black snake.

"Go find Pax. Senor Bennett." Her voice shook. Understandable, considering the terror racing through her system.

As Celia ran off, Sage kept her eyes locked on the evil reptile. She had to make sure he didn't slither off and attack any of the many groups working nearby in the schoolyard. Thankfully, the snake seemed more interested in resting between the rocks than launching into a murderous assault. To be honest, aside from poking his head from the crack in the rocks to look around a little, he didn't move much, obviously unthreatened by her.

She wished she felt the same.

Jeez-o-Pete! Sir Hiss had probably been watching her work all day. That disturbing little realization sent a shudder of earthquake proportions down her spine. Her fingers turned numb and vision started to haze at the edges. Deep breaths. She needed to get her heart rate out of the red zone. If she passed out now, the evil serpent would probably slither back and forth across her prostrate body.

She sucked in breaths through her nose and blew out through her mouth, praying snakes with black bodies and iridescent green and yellow spots weren't poisonous. Her nemesis swayed his head from side to side and tested the air with his tongue, but he never broke eye contact. She couldn't win this staring contest—she was sure to blink first. Did snakes even have eyelids? Sweat trickled down her neck. Where the hell was Pax?

She lifted her right foot and slowly lowered it one step behind her. Unfortunately, her foot landed on top of the spade she'd set down when she'd first made the brilliant decision to move the rocks by herself. She stumbled backward, thudding to a noisy stop against the pot of the unplanted bush.

Chest tight, she checked on Sir Hiss. Holy Buckets! He slithered from the rocks and was heading straight at her. Her instincts screamed *run*! But hadn't she heard snakes would chase you if you ran from them? Or was that bears? A flood of panic and adrenaline coursed through her, washing away coherent thought.

"Don't move," Pax ordered from behind her.

Not a problem. The snake was only a few feet away, and fear and indecision made movement virtually impossible.

In a blur of motion, Pax charged past her and snagged the three-foot snake with his gloved hand. He held Hiss a few inches below his head, grasping him about halfway down his body with the other hand.

"Are you okay?" he asked, concern edging his voice.

"Uh-huh." She nodded, her eyes remaining on Hiss.

"You look pale."

"Uh-huh."

"It's okay. It's just a racer. He's harmless."

"Uh-huh."

"Sage, honey, can you please say something else?" Pax's soothing voice broke through the fog settling around her.

She shook her head and broke eye contact with Hiss. She raised her gaze to find Pax's searching brown eyes locked on hers. "What are you"—she cleared her dry throat—"going to do with him?"

"I'll carry this guy to Logan to relocate somewhere far from the school. Hang tight. I'll be right back."

Sage clenched her jaw. She was so damn sick of being afraid. Afraid of snakes. Afraid of taking risks. Afraid of jeopardizing her boring, stable existence.

How did she get here? How did fear take over her life and she not even notice?

She huffed out a breath and squared her shoulders. "I'll do it."

"What?" Pax's brows arched upward.

"I'll carry the snake to Logan." She tipped her chin up. "I'm so done being afraid. It's not poisonous. It can't do any real harm, yet I'm shaking like a squirrel at a dog park." She held up an unsteady hand to prove the point. "Maybe if I carry the stupid thing, I won't get so freaked out the next time I see one."

Pax studied her, his eyes focused and assessing, seemingly unconcerned about the wriggling snake in his hands. After a long pause, he shrugged a shoulder. "Okay."

"That's it? You're not going to try to talk me out of it? What if I hyperventilate, pass out, go into cardiac arrest, or all of the above?" Her voice rose in volume and pitch with each word.

"Do you want me to talk you out of carrying the snake to Logan?"

She blew out a breath. "Of course I want you to talk me out of it, but I'm going to do it anyway."

Pax grinned. "Okay. Here you go." He extended his arms, the movement making Sir Hiss struggle in his grasp.

Sage jumped back a step and held up her hands. "Whoa, slow down. I've got to prepare for this little adventure."

After slipping on a thick pair of work gloves and indulging in a full body heebie-jeebies shiver, she stepped forward. "Now I'm ready."

Pax slowly maneuvered the snake toward her. "Hold him firmly with one hand right behind his head and the other about halfway down his body. Walk him slowly to the parking lot. Logan is working there."

Heart racing, Sage wrapped her shaking fingers around Hiss's body. The snake squirmed in her hands, fighting his restraints. *Eww* and double *eww*.

She clenched her jaw. She needed to find Logan before she freaked out.

She hustled toward the parking lot, arms stretched as far in front of her as possible. She mumbled an embarrassing string of obscenities under her breath and fought the nearly overwhelming urge to chuck the snake to the ground and run away screaming.

Some small part of her registered that a number of the volunteers were watching her. Her heart pounded and blood rushed in her ears. When she finally reached the parking lot, she stopped abruptly and managed to croak out, "Logan?"

She couldn't do this much longer. She'd either faint or throw the stupid snake if she didn't find Logan soon.

She felt two strong hands settle on her shoulders.

"He's by the truck. Come on. You're almost there," Pax said quietly behind her.

She'd been so focused on Hiss she hadn't realized Pax was right there with her all along. Carrying an evil serpent of death could really screw with your senses.

She gulped and focused on the warmth seeping into her cold skin where his hands rested on her shoulders.

Pax steered her toward a beat-up red truck parked near the entrance. Logan stood in the bed of the truck, lowering potted plants to Brick and a few other volunteers. A frown settled between his eyes as he watched her approach. "Whoa, darl, did you bring me a present?" In one fluid movement, he jumped from the truck bed and hustled toward her.

"*Uhnf.*"

Logan scooped the snake from her death grip and lifted Hiss to eye level for a closer inspection. "Ah, she's a beauty. Look at the coloration."

Sage stumbled backward and bumped to a halt against Pax. He slid his hands from her shoulders to her upper arms and gently settled her against his chest. Warmth rushed into her body, his nearness giving her strength.

"You're as white as a ghost and shaking like a wet kitten," Logan said. He smirked in Pax's direction. "Mate, you really know how to show a lady a good time."

FIFTEEN

"NOW that you're on friendly terms with our no-legged friends of the jungle, I don't need to hang around here and protect you anymore." Kat pulled a pair of pajamas from a drawer and tucked them into the small bag draped over her shoulder. "I'm going to hang with Mom at Pax's house tonight. We're going to watch Carter O'Reilly's newest movie." She turned back to Sage and fanned her face with a slow, exaggerated motion. "That man is beyond hot."

"I didn't realize you'd been protecting me the last few nights," Sage said, an eyebrow raised.

"Totally. I knew how freaked you were by the opening in the shower, and reptiles don't bother me. Figured I'd play the knight in shining armor if a snake crawled through the opening. But no need now that you know exactly how to escort one of those little bastards from the room."

"You realize I'm only slightly less afraid of snakes, right? I assure you, if one tries to join me in the shower, I still plan to run away screaming, just not quite as fast or quite as loud as I would have yesterday."

"Even a little bit of progress is progress," Kat said with a wry smile. "Seriously. You did good today, babe. I didn't think you had it in you."

Sage shook her head and shuddered. "Neither did I. I still can't believe I touched a snake, let alone carried it miles through the jungles of Costa Rica."

"Miles?" Kat said with a look that perfectly married skepticism and sympathy.

"Okay, fine. I carried a harmless snake through a playground for a few yards." Sage blew out a breath. "Trust me, it seemed a lot more dramatic at the time. Not that you could understand. You're such a badass. You're not afraid of anything."

A shadow crossed Kat's delicate features. "We're all afraid of something."

Sage had expected a flippant response. Kat's serious tone didn't gel with her usual exuberance. "I wish you'd tell me what's wrong."

In an instant, the shadow cleared and Kat's face lit up with a teasing smile. "You're keeping me from my movie date with Mr. O'Reilly, that's what's wrong." Her friend pulled her in for a quick hug. "Gotta run. I'll catch you for a good-bye before your flight tomorrow. And I hope any unexpected visitors tonight are of the extremely enjoyable kind."

With a wink, Kat slipped from the room.

"Jeez," Sage muttered. Guess she was more transparent than she'd realized. Hopefully, no one else could read her as easily as her best friend. She didn't know what she would say if Will or any of the Bennetts questioned her about her feelings toward Pax.

She slid open the glass door leading to the wooden deck that wrapped around the villa and stepped out into the moonlit night. Hands braced on the railing, she focused on the lapping waves and gentle breeze as she filled her lungs with deep breaths. She would miss the fresh, salty scent of the ocean and the soothing sounds of the jungle around her. She would miss the tranquility, the beauty, the adventure, and the unexpected contentment she'd found here. And, most of all she would miss Pax.

It seemed strange to think that this time tomorrow, she'd be back in her characterless apartment in a suburb outside of Milwaukee. Rather than views of the ocean, her apartment looked over a parking lot and onto another apartment building that varied from her own in no significant way.

Rather than the sounds of nocturnal animals and rustling foliage, tomorrow she would be listening to the muted sounds of her neighbors' television sets, an occasional siren wailing in the distance, and the regular slamming of car doors in the parking lot as other people lived their lives. Her life in Milwaukee was stable, safe, and predictable—everything she'd always wanted.

So why did the thought of going home depress her so much?

She shifted her eyes, looking for anything to distract her. She spotted a familiar male figure walking along the beach alone.

Okay, so what if for the first time ever she now questioned whether the plan she'd devised and carefully followed every day of her life could actually lead to happiness? That only meant she might have screwed up her own life and had no idea how to straighten it back out. It didn't mean she shouldn't try to fix other people's issues. Right?

This was her chance. Without even stopping to slip on shoes, she rushed down the stairs and onto the beach, slowing only when she reached the side of the tall man.

"Hi, Mr. Bennett. Mind if I join you?"

Richard Bennett turned to look at her, the nearly full moon illuminating the smile on his handsome features. Though Sage had attended his sixtieth birthday a couple of years earlier, he appeared to be in better shape than a lot of men half his age. Pax might have issues with his dad, but passing down crappy genes sure wasn't one of them.

"Good evening, Sage. I'd love for you to join me. I had to get away for a while. My wife and daughter are planning to ogle some Hollywood hunk tonight. It's rather uncomfortable to watch."

She grinned. "I can imagine that would be awkward for you. I'm sorry to say what I want to talk with you about might be even more uncomfortable."

"Are you going to discuss the hardness of some guy's abs?"

"I promise not to mention any part of the male anatomy."

"You have my gratitude." He smiled warmly down at her. "What did you want to talk about?"

Sage took a deep breath and squared her shoulders, carefully preparing what she wanted to say to the man who'd opened his home and his heart to her time and again.

"I've always admired many things about you," she said slowly. "You're a great leader and an excellent businessman. You have a strong moral compass, and you show respect to anyone who deserves it, even those less wealthy or powerful than you."

"I'm going to start blushing if you keep this up." Richard turned his head toward the water. "It's really not necessary for you to sing my praises."

Sage laid her hand on his arm, forcing him to turn his attention back to her. "It never mattered to you that I grew up with a single mom far from the upper-echelons of society where you moved. You welcomed me into your home again and again over the years, showing me only kindness and generosity. On top of everything else, I'm well aware that Pembrock Bank hired me after the referral you insisted on giving in person."

"You really don't have to say all this." Richard patted her hand. "I think of you like one of my daughters."

"And you are the father I always wanted. So please know what I'm about to say is coming from a place of love." She gave him a steely-eyed look and poked an index finger into his chest. "You're acting like a butthead."

Richard's head snapped back. "Excuse me?"

"I didn't say you are a butthead. I said you are acting like a butthead." She dropped her hands to her hips and stretched to her full height. "Pax is an amazing man who takes after his father in all the ways I mentioned a minute ago. The community respects him, and his employees are as loyal as they are hardworking. His business runs at capacity the entire year and has a higher return on investment than yours." She paused to catch her breath. "As soon as you stop acting like a butthead, you'll realize you should not only be supportive of the life your son has built here, you should be damn proud of it."

His features went emotionless. Her gut clenched, and she realized that she might have crossed a line, but she meant everything she'd said and didn't regret saying it.

Sage pinned him with her narrowed gaze.

After a long, tense minute, Richard's rigid posture crumbled as he let out a breath. "You may be right." He raked a hand down his face. "The rub is, I've known that what you just said is true for a while now, but I can't change the past. Even if I say I'm sorry, that does nothing to change what was done and what was said years ago."

"So don't worry about fixing the past. Life isn't a sitcom. You can't clean up all the junk that has happened before in thirty quick minutes." She shifted her weight to her right leg and tilted her head to the side as she looked up at Richard with her most encouraging expression. "Focus on making the future better. Pax is moving forward with his life. He's building his future here, and you can ask to be a part of that future. Isn't the potential return worth the risk of rejection?"

Richard's eyes lit in unexpected humor as a smile tilted the corners of his mouth. "Thank you, Sage." He cupped her shoulders in his hands and planted a fatherly kiss on her forehead. "It's funny," he said, stepping back. "Sometimes another's advice is perfect. And sometimes our advice for another is also the perfect advice for ourselves." He gave her a quick wink. "Goodnight, sweetheart."

"Huh?" Perplexed, Sage watched him turn around and walk toward the path leading to Pax's house. What a cryptic response...

Jeez-o-Pete! She sucked in a breath and jolted to attention. Richard knew. He knew how she felt about his son. Her cheeks heated as she sank down to the sand and rested her forearms on her bent knees, staring blindly out to the sea. Looked like she'd done a crappy job keeping her emotions to herself.

A rustling of leaves and a sense of something moving drew her attention to the jungle. "Pax, is that you?" She rose to her feet, dusted the sand from her sundress, and squinted in the direction of the noise.

"Are you expecting him?" Will stepped into view on the dimly lit path leading from his villa to the water's edge.

"Oh, hi. No, I wasn't expecting Pax. Why would I be?" Sage's laugh rang falsely in her ears.

"I'm no fool. I can see something is going on between the two of you." Will stopped next to her, a condescending expression on his lean face. "I assume it's some sort of fling. God knows Paxton Bennett is not the kind of man to commit to anyone."

"That's not true."

"Which part?"

"Any of it," Sage snapped. "We're not having a fling, and Pax can commit."

"Has he offered you a commitment?"

"Well. No. But look how devoted he is to La Vida. He's willing to do anything to keep her."

"Such as sleeping with his loan officer."

"I did not sleep with him! And even if I had, it wouldn't have anything to do with his loan." She flung her arms in the air for emphasis.

"There's no need for dramatics." Will gave a lofty sigh. "You're a good girl. I don't blame any of this on you."

"What the hell does that mean?"

He raised an eyebrow. "It means I'm sure you had no idea of his true intentions. I still think we make a smart couple. Once you distance yourself from this situation, I'm sure you'll agree."

Sage stepped back and looked at him, her mouth hanging open. "Let me get this straight. You think I've been having sex with Pax this week, and you'd still like to date me?"

"No one at home knows what happened here. Of course, I would insist on monogamy once we return to Wisconsin. Without it, our image would be irrevocable damaged."

"Our image?" Sage gaped.

"I'll be taking over my father's bank soon, and Richard Bennett has taken on the role of surrogate father to you. If we marry, that combination would bring us both a lot of prestige and influence."

"Marry?" Shock radiated through her. "You want to marry me because of my connection to the Bennetts?" Un. Be. Lievable. "Aren't you afraid Richard and Ann would be angry if you steal me from their son?" she asked dryly.

"Maybe, if he actually wanted you for the long run." Will smirked. "Has he mentioned marriage?"

She clamped her mouth shut and narrowed her eyes.

"I didn't think so," Will said, a note of pity in his voice. "We'll discuss this after we return home and your head is clear. You'll realize everything I've said is well thought out and logical. And we both know, that's exactly how you like things."

Sage cursed under her breath and stomped her foot in the sand as Will left. Damn him for trying to use logic to justify his ridiculous proposal. There was nothing logical about walking away from the man she loved to marry a man who cared more about image than he did her.

Whoa. Back up. She loved Pax?

Her heart swelled with emotion, and she felt a goofy, I've-got-it-bad smile spread across her face.

Yep. With a complete disregard to logic, she'd fallen madly, stupidly in love with Paxton Bennett.

SIXTEEN

SAGE sucked in air at the back of Pax's yard and fought to get her heart rate under control. She'd run the entire way up the private trail from the beach to Pax's home. The fact that she was barefoot and might step on a snake as she ran the jungle path had kept her pace at near Olympian levels. Carrying a snake with gloves was one thing, but the possibility of stepping on one in the dark upped the ick factor to a near hyperventilating level.

Once she caught her breath, she looked across the backyard to the dimly lit outdoor seating area around the pool. She saw the silhouette of Pax sitting in one of the chairs. She squinted through the darkness, hoping to make out if he was alone. As if sensing her gaze, he rose from the chair and began walking straight toward her.

Sage took another deep breath and continued to watch as his lithe gait carried him closer. Only Pax moved with equal amounts of power and grace. Her body tightened in anticipation.

Falling in love with Pax had made her finally understand that the lonely existence she'd created for herself was more dangerous than risking her heart. She couldn't stand looking back on her life fifty years from now and realizing she'd turned down every adventure life had offered her. She wanted to laugh, cry, dream, love.

She wanted to truly live.

A broken heart would heal. A life full of regrets would kill her.

Pax stopped directly in front of her, eyebrows raised and a smile tugging the corners of his lips. "Out for an evening stroll?" He scanned her body, tilting his head to the side when he reached her feet. "Barefoot?"

"It's a long story."

"Do I want to know?"

"Definitely not."

"There is something I'm curious about." He tipped his head toward her and raised one eyebrow. "My dad just cornered me into having a little talk. Do you know anything about that?"

"That depends." Sage shifted her weight from one bare foot to the other. "How'd the talk go?"

A spark of humor lit his eyes and the corner of his lips twitched. All good signs in her opinion.

Pax studied the darkened jungle behind her. "He said I had done a good job with La Vida, and he asked if he and Mom could visit again soon." He turned his head to look out over the ocean, still not meeting her eyes. "He also wants to help out financially. He offered to cosign for the loan. He said it would be a shame to lose this place." He paused and swallowed hard. "He even mentioned a few ideas about constructing a spa here for guests to enjoy after a day of adventure activities or volunteering."

"Pax, that's great news." Sage placed her hand on his cheek and turned his head toward her. She saw reluctance and embarrassment in his expression. "He's proud of you. I'm thrilled he's finally found a way to let you know that."

"He didn't actually say the word proud any time during the talk."

"People don't usually tell you exactly how they feel. And sometimes it's harder to actually say a word than it is to show it." Sage aimed her most persuasive smile in his direction. "Now how about a piggyback ride back to my villa? You know, for old times' sake."

"Old times' sake, my ass." Pax gave her a devilish grin of his own. "You're afraid of stepping on a snake in the dark."

"Hey, I've already had one run-in with a serpent of death today. I'm not sure I would survive another."

"Fine." Pax scooped her up, swung her around to his back, and started down the path to her villa. "Just try not to strangle me this time."

"Yes, sir." Sage wrapped her arms around him and clung tightly to his shoulders. Holy buckets, he felt good. Breasts pressed to his back, she wiggled to get even closer. And he smelled amazing. She buried her face in the back of his neck and inhaled the warm, masculine scent of soap and sun-browned, salty skin. Desire burned through her.

"Did you just purr?" he asked in a strained voice.

"Uh-huh." She took another deep breath. "Can't help it."

She licked his neck.

"Are you trying to torture me?"

"Actually, the things I'm thinking about doing to you should feel good... really, really good." She licked up his neck to the lobe of his ear where she decided to use the tip of her tongue.

Pax moaned deep in his throat and nearly flew up the stairs with her and into her villa. He slammed the door shut behind them and swung her around. He caught her mouth with his own in a demanding kiss and pressed her against the door.

She clung to him, her arms around his neck and her legs around his waist. Her sundress rode up to the top of her thighs, leaving only a lacy pair of panties between her and the rough denim of his jeans. She pulled him closer and pushed against him with her hips, trying to find relief from the exquisite torture.

"We have to stop," Pax said, tearing his mouth from hers.

Fear tightened her chest. She needed to be with him, if not forever, then at least for tonight. "I don't want to stop."

"I'm trying to do the right thing." His voice sounded thick, almost desperate.

"Tonight, us being together is the right thing."

"And tomorrow?"

"I don't know." Sage shook her head. "All I know is that I'm tired of worrying about the future. For once in my life, I just want to live in the moment."

Pax remained motionless, his gaze locked on hers for a tension-filled moment. Finally, she felt a shudder run through him, and he gave up the fight. Slowly, tenderly he claimed her mouth.

Desire flooded her. She squirmed in his arms and deepened the kiss. "Please, Pax. I need you. Now."

"Soon. Not yet," he said, his voice rough. "I've waited too long to rush this."

He carried her to the bedroom, laid her gently on the bed, and stretched out alongside her. She threaded her fingers through his dark hair, holding him to her as he spent countless minutes feathering kisses along her neck and shoulders. After he'd kissed every bare inch of her skin, he slid the slim straps from her shoulders and lowered her dress, leaving her naked to the waist. When he rolled one pebbled nipple between his thumb and index finger, she moaned.

"God, you're beautiful." He lowered his head and pulled her nipple into his mouth.

Jolts of electricity shot through her, scorched her nerve endings, and set off an ache low in her belly. She squirmed as he leisurely sucked, nipped, kissed, and teased her with his lips.

"Pax," she moaned, reaching for him, unable to stand the torment any longer.

"Hmm?" he murmured, then caught her nipple between his teeth.

"Too many clothes." She pulled frantically at his shirt, needing him naked.

He slipped from her reach, trailing kisses down her body and sliding the rest of her clothes to the floor.

She propped herself on her elbows and narrowed her eyes. "I meant that you had too many clothes on."

He stood and stripped off his shirt and jeans. "You're not very patient." He grinned down at her.

"Not very patient?" Her belly tightened as her eyes roamed over his hard, lean muscles. "I've wanted this for six years."

Pax's grin widened. "That's good to know."

He rejoined her on the bed and pulled her close as her skin hummed with excitement and anticipation. He trailed kisses from the curve of her neck to the sensitive spot behind her ear, while his hands moved lower, exploring. She gasped when he finally pushed two fingers into her wetness.

"I've wanted you a lot longer than six years," he murmured, kissing her neck and working his fingers in and out.

She cried out, arching her back and rolling her hips against his hand. "I need you. In me. Now." She panted, clutching his shoulders and thrashing beneath him, desperate for more.

"You first," Pax murmured.

"Not without you." She reached down and wrapped her fingers around him.

He sucked in a breath and then moaned as she moved her hand along his length. "You win," he said, his features tight as he fought for control.

In a blissful haze, Sage watched him slide on a condom and position himself between her thighs. He leaned forward to take her mouth in another tender kiss and slowly, steadily pushed inside of her.

Buried to her core, he stilled, gripping her hip to keep her from moving. "You feel so damn good." He pulled out and pushed in again. "Too good to be real."

He set a slow, torturous pace. Thrusting and withdrawing almost completely before thrusting back into her. With each plunge, she clung tighter and moaned with pleasure as his length stroked deep inside of her.

His eyes burned into her as he slid his hand from her hip, pressed his thumb firmly onto the hard nub at her center, and circled twice. Just as she almost sailed over the edge, he pulled his hand away.

"Don't stop!" she begged, writhing under him. "Please!"

"Sage!" Her name ripped from his lips, and his restraint disappeared. He slammed wildly into her while his thumb pushed and circled her sensitive flesh.

She exploded in wave after wave of pleasure. She panted and pulsed around him. He tensed and then slammed into her one final time.

"Sage!" He came with a raw, gruff sound of pure masculine satisfaction.

She smiled. She was exactly where she wanted to be.

•••

Sage woke in the night to the sound of the gently whirling ceiling fan and the distant calls of jungle animals. She recognized the comfort of her bed, but the unfamiliar pressure on her chest took a moment to identify. Pax had thrown a muscular arm across her while they slept. She snuggled closer against his chest, loving the heavy weight of his arm and his rhythmic breathing against her cheek.

Being next to him made her feel cherished and cared for and not alone for the first time in memory. Her mom had been so addicted to the high of attracting a new man that she'd too often focused her efforts on the opposite sex rather than the needs of the household she shared with her daughter. Sage had started picking up the slack at an early age.

Somewhere along the way, the burden of responsibility had caused her to trade living a full life for living a safe one. But not anymore. She couldn't go back to the lonely, secure, independent life she'd accepted in the past. Pax had taught her the beauty of following a dream, and he'd inspired her to fight for hers.

She rolled to her side to face the man she loved.

No fear.

"Pax," she whispered. "Hey. You awake?"

"Mmm," he murmured, tightening his hold around her, pulling her even closer. "I can be if you need me again." Though his eyes remained closed, a wicked smile spread across his face.

Sage's belly tightened in response. How could a smile be sleepy and sinful at the same time?

"Funny you mention it," she said in an unnaturally high voice. She took a breath to calm her jittery nerves and started again. "I do need you. That's what I've finally realized. I need your strength. I need your kindness. I need your dedication, determination, and drive to do the right thing. Most of all, I need your help to be who I want to be, an adventurous person who embraces life rather than avoids it."

Pax's eyes snapped open and burned into her with an unrecognizable mixture of emotions. Well, not completely unrecognizable. She could read his shock clearly, and maybe a little panic as well. But there were other, darker flashes in his eyes she couldn't make out.

She fought against the fear clawing at her gut. She'd decided to reach for her dream and wouldn't stop now.

"You don't need me," he said briskly, breaking eye contact and climbing from the bed. "My life here doesn't fit into your plans. Yeah, the sex was amazing. But don't throw your future away because of an orgasm." He blew out a breath, ran a rough hand through his hair, and then quickly grabbed his pants from the dark floor.

Sage sat up, clutching the sheet to her chest. She watched him step into the jeans and knew she was about to lose him. But she refused to quit.

No fear.

"It's not about the sex."

He looked at her, skepticism etched in every detail of his face.

"I love—"

"No," he interrupted. "Don't say it."

She jerked back at his emotionless tone. She clutched the sheets painfully over her heart and swallowed back the sudden lump in her throat.

She loved his courage and his strength to fight for his dream. Now she needed to be strong. She could never forgive herself if she walked away without risking everything.

No fear.

"I love you. I've always loved you, Pax." Her heart squeezed. She tipped her head back and sniffled in a useless attempt to stop the tears from spilling over. When the first drop slid down her cheek, she pulled her shoulders back, drew in a deep breath, and attempted a shaky smile on the exhale. "Always will."

For a moment, emotion flashed across his face and burned through his eyes. But an instant later it was gone, leaving only a hardened expression. And while he stood motionless staring down on her, she knew her time with him was over. She knew by the tension of his stance and by the cold, hard look in his eyes. Yeah, she knew.

She'd already lost him.

"Go home, Sage. There's nothing for you here."

No tremor shook his voice, no remorse faltered his step. He simply turned and walked away from her, disappearing silently into the darkness. Out of her life.

SEVENTEEN

"YOU wanted to see me, Will?" Sage stepped into her boss's sterile corner office near the end of another long day at work.

Outside the expansive windows, a winter storm howled with fury, blowing and whipping snow vertically across the landscape. A lot of her coworkers at Pembrock Bank had left at lunchtime to avoid the worst of the storm. Not wanting to get trapped at home, alone with her thoughts, Sage had decided to risk the weather and stay until closing.

She'd left Costa Rica a week ago. While she missed the warmth of the tropics, she missed Pax even more. She missed his smile and his strength. She missed being with someone who knew her a little better than she knew herself. She still ached at the thought of him. And since she thought about him every other minute, she ached a lot.

"Have a seat." Will motioned to the leather chair in front of his desk. "I wanted an update on Paxton Bennett's loan."

Pushing away the pain of hearing his name, Sage sat down and did her best to focus on the man in front of her. "I finished work on it today. His parents' backing guaranteed the loan's approval. I sent an email to let him know."

"Excellent. I'm glad it worked out so smoothly. I know the Bennetts said they didn't expect us to approve the loan as a favor, but I still feared they'd be disappointed if we denied it." Will sat back in his chair. "I'm also glad to hear he will remain in Costa Rica. We don't need that type of... distraction here."

Ha! Pax didn't need to be close to be a distraction. The tight knot in her chest told her it didn't matter how much distance or time she put between them. He would always be in her thoughts and, worse, he would be permanently entrenched in her stupid, idiotic heart.

"Now that you're away from there, I was hoping you've thought about my offer with the sensible perspective that distance brings."

She cocked an eyebrow. "You mean treating marriage like a business venture? I can't do that. Marriage should be a venture of the heart."

"Don't be so dramatic," Will said with a condescending expression. "I can give you what you've always wanted. A good life and a solid marriage."

"But not love?"

"Love fades."

"Not if you're doing it right," Sage said on a sigh.

He rolled his eyes. "I didn't take you for a romantic."

"You're right. What you're offering is what I always wanted for my future." Sage closed her eyes for a beat. "But not anymore. I want more out of life. I'm sorry, Will, but my answer is no. Oh, and I quit." She stood to leave, the gratifying conviction that she'd made the right—the *brave*—decision lifting her heart for the first time in a week.

She wouldn't spend her life in a crappy marriage and an unfulfilling job just because the guy she loved didn't love her back. She would move to Silver Bay and find a job that fulfilled her. Sure, without Pax her life would never be perfect. But she would damn well make it better than it was right now.

"Quit? You're willing to throw everything away, even your future?" Will asked in disbelief.

"I haven't lost my future. I finally intend to find it."

•••

Pax sat tense, miserable, and motionless in his office at La Vida. He'd almost grown used to the darkness engulfing him since pushing Sage from his life a week earlier, but a fresh wave of pain had kicked his ass when he received an email from her earlier in the day. He'd been scrutinizing the message for hours, desperate to read something between the lines. Problem was, she'd only written one damn line.

La Vida's loan has been approved. -Sage

He scowled at the screen. He should be thrilled by the news. Two weeks ago, he would have been. Two weeks ago, securing money for La Vida's future had been the only thing he'd wanted in life. How in the hell had everything gone to shit in two weeks?

"I'd be pissed at you if you weren't so damn pathetic." Kat leaned against his office doorway, her expression and tone matching her black attire. "I just called Sage. She told me what you said to her. What the hell were you thinking? She tells you that she loves you. And you do what? You frickin' tell her to go home. You're an idiot."

"There's nothing for her here."

"Don't give me that crap. You're here." She pointed an accusing finger at him. "And you love her. Everyone knows it. We all saw the sappy sentiment written on your face every time you looked at her."

His eyes widened in surprise. She had to be exaggerating. He couldn't have been that obvious. Okay, Kat had figured it out, and possibly Logan. But no way anyone else knew.

"Even Brick saw right through you." Kat smirked as if reading his mind. "He said you looked at her like she was 'prettier than a glob of butter melting on a stack of pancakes,' whatever the hell that means."

He blew out a resigned breath. "Fine. I love her. And that's exactly why I told her to go home. I wasn't lying, Kat. There is nothing for her here. I couldn't let her throw her future away for me."

"So you think she's better off with a guy like Will Pembrock?"

"Shit, no. He doesn't understand her."

Kat raised an eyebrow. "And you do?"

"I understand that Sage deserves everything she has always wanted, and that includes finding a compatible guy to marry and put down roots with in Wisconsin. She wants a traditional life with a traditional husband." Pax spat the words in frustration. "But that's not who I am, and it's not who I'm ever going to be. If she gives up everything to be with me, what happens when she wakes up one morning and realizes she made a huge mistake?" He scrubbed a hand down his face. "I don't want to become her biggest regret."

"You're such an idiot. Yeah, she wants stability. But did you ever bother asking her what that means to her?"

He narrowed his eyes and tipped his head to the side, wondering where this was going.

"I didn't think so." Kat rolled her eyes. "Sage doesn't give a damn where she lives or if her husband works at some stuffy office. She simply wants to build a future with a man who loves her. She wants to be part of something special and to be loved by someone special. That's all." Kat paused. "You, and the life you've built here, can give her that."

Pax swallowed hard.

"Deep in your gut, you know I'm right. Now stop being a dumbass. Go tell her how you feel and what you really want."

What if being with him at La Vida could really be enough to make Sage happy in the long run? His heart expanded at the future Kat dangled in front of him. A future that would be much brighter with Sage in it. "Do you know where she is?" he asked quickly.

A cunning smile spread across Kat's face. "I don't know where she is right now, but I do know where she's going."

EIGHTEEN

A week after quitting her job, Sage pulled her reliable Toyota sedan into the only open space in front of Silver Bay's new coffee shop, Fresh. It sat two blocks from Lake Michigan on the historic downtown square. Judging by the number of full tables she saw through the large windows spanning the front and wrapping around the side of the building, Fresh was a hit.

Sage found the small Help Wanted sign posted in the lower corner of the window even more interesting than the café's obvious popularity. Working in a coffee house couldn't financially compete with her former job, but it could pay the bills while she figured out a new path for her life.

In less than a month, she'd given her heart to a man who didn't want it, quit her stable job at the bank, sublet her apartment, and driven to Silver Bay with no new employment and no place to live. At least people could no longer call her boring or overly cautious.

She'd even accomplished the amazing feat of rendering Kat speechless for a full thirty seconds when she'd called her in Costa Rica last week to tell her about quitting her job. Excited to hear the news, Kat had insisted on helping Sage find at least temporary employment.

It had been Kat's idea for Sage to stop by the coffee shop. Kat knew the woman who owned the café and thought it would be a perfect fit for Sage during her "transition to greatness," as her best friend liked to refer to the emotion-inducing adventures Sage had lived through in the past few weeks.

Sage pushed through the café's glass door, and an old-fashioned bell rang overhead. The enticing aroma of rich coffee and fresh pastries filled the air with a heavenly scent. She drew in a deep breath and grinned, taking in the eccentric atmosphere.

The original brick walls showcased the bold, bright, and playful artwork. Tables and comfortable-looking chairs of different sizes, shapes, and finishes filled the space. A trio of high-tech and complicated-looking coffee machines sat on the old-fashioned counter at the back of the store in a harmonious contradiction. The owner had blended a variety of decorating styles, but somehow it all worked.

Fresh, the newest addition to Silver Bay, embodied whimsical perfection.

A few heads turned to look at her hesitating in the doorway. Sage recognized most of the customers as longtime Silver Bay residents. She squared her shoulders, smiled in acknowledgment, and received welcoming nods and smiles in return.

"Hi, Sage."

Sage looked in the direction of the familiar voice. "Hannah? You're the owner?"

"Yep."

Leave it to Kat to omit the fact that her older sister owned Fresh.

The lovely brunette stepped from around the counter with her arms outstretched. As they hugged, Hannah whispered, "No matter what happens, you need to know that I'll always be your friend, and I'll always be here for you."

Sage leaned back and eyed Hannah. "Cryptic much?"

Hannah's expression grew serious, and she shifted her gaze to the back of the shop.

Holy buckets.

Pax sat at a table tucked in the corner of the café. His eyes locked on hers, intensity and apprehension pouring off him in waves. Her chest tightened at the sight of him, and Sage fought to breathe. She clenched her suddenly numb fingers as he unfolded his long, lean frame from the small table and began moving toward her.

She forced in a deep, calming breath. She needed to slow her heart's frantic beat before she fainted like some weak-kneed damsel in distress.

"Pax. I had no idea you were in town." She choked out the words, hoping she managed an almost normal tone. "Seriously, I'm not stalking you. I'll come back later." She turned and bolted for the door, desperate to get away before she starred in a pathetic unrequited love scene on a very public stage.

"Sage, wait. Please. Can we talk?"

She couldn't. Not yet. She needed more time to heal before she could face him again. Maybe someday they could be friends. Maybe someday seeing him wouldn't pierce her heart. But not yet. Not today.

Without looking back, she gave a small shake of her head, flung the door open, and rushed blindly out of the café.

•••

Damn it. He had to catch her. Cursing under his breath, Pax fought his way through the collection of mismatched tables scattered through the coffee shop like a damn tea party obstacle course. He bumped into the back of some guy's chair, mumbled a distracted apology, and glared at his blasted sister for not leaving enough space for a guy to maneuver through. Finally stepping around the last table, he charged for the door.

Hannah stepped in front of him. "Hold it right there," she ordered, placing her hand on his chest.

"What?" He ground out the word, fighting down the temptation to push past her.

"You've sat in that chair from opening to closing for five days and the best line you can come up with is 'Can we talk?' That's just embarrassing." Hannah rolled her eyes in a dramatic display of his epic failure. "I'm not a romantic like Claire. And even though I think most women would be better off without a guy messing up her life, I allowed you to wait here because Kat promised me that you loved Sage and wanted to set things right. But if that was your attempt at professing your undying love... well, frankly, she might be better off without you."

He pinned her with a murderous look, frustration and desperation clawing at his gut. "If you're done lecturing me, I'd like to find Sage before I lose her again."

"You have to do more than find her, brother. You have to convince her that you deserve her. I don't know how you'll do that if you don't even believe it yourself." Her soft words hit harder than a fist.

"I have to try."

She dropped her hand from his chest and stepped out of his path. "She turned toward the water. I'm sure you can find her by the shore."

He rushed out the door and braced himself against the frigid wind blowing off the lake as he headed to the water's edge. Hannah was right. Catching up to Sage wouldn't be enough. Apologizing and admitting his love might not be enough to make up for hurting her either, but after living the past weeks in the suffocating fog of blackness and misery, he wasn't giving up without a fight.

His long strides quickly ate up the two blocks from Hannah's café to the lake. Once he crossed over the wide bike path that edged the town's beach, he saw her. She stood near the surf, her concentration focused on the turbulent waves hammering the icy shore.

His tension lessened with each step he took toward her. Even knowing she might tell him to go to hell, he still craved the contentment being near her brought.

Sage stood facing the lake with her arms wrapped tightly across her body. She didn't turn to face him when he stopped next to her. Instead, her body tensed. It killed him that she needed to brace herself just to talk to him. Not that he blamed her. He'd hurt her in Costa Rica. He'd purposely pushed her away, and he knew it might be too late for him to do a damn thing about it.

•••

Sage locked her arms tighter around her body in a useless defense against the tidal wave of emotions Pax's nearness triggered in her.

"I told you to go home because I was afraid," he said, his voice gravel-rough. "Not afraid of loving you. I've never been afraid of that. I started falling for you all those years ago here in Silver Bay."

Eyes wide, she turned to look at him. His hands were shoved into his front pockets. Everything about him from his rigid stance to his pleading eyes radiated a level of anxiety she'd never seen in him before.

"You pushed me away then too," she said.

"Because my life was two thousand miles away, a life I couldn't imagine you'd ever want. I couldn't ask you to give up your life in Wisconsin to be with me then, and I couldn't do it when you were at La Vida either. When you said you loved me and would give up everything for me, I panicked. It would kill me to become your biggest regret."

Her heart squeezed. She unfolded her arms, stepped closer, and laid a hand on his arm. She ached to ease his pain but remained silent, unsure of what to say.

"I love you." Emotion deepened his voice and shook his words. "It's not a secret. Hell, everybody at La Vida figured it out within a few days. Apparently, even Brick realized it, and he once thought the vacuum cleaner was a giant Transformer." Pax shook his head and shot her a self-conscious smile. "Sorry, now I'm the one who's rambling. I've never told a woman I love her before." He shoved a hand through his hair. "It's terrifying."

Sage bit her lip as hope lifted her heart and threatened to spread a goofy smile across her face. "Pax—"

"Wait. There's more I need to say." He took her hands in his. "I used to believe La Vida was all I needed in life, but that's not true. I'll never be content unless you're by my side. Move to La Vida and build a future with me there. Or I'll move to Silver Bay if you'd rather." He squeezed her hands tighter. "I don't care where I am as long as I'm with you."

Her heart expended with so much joy and excitement she thought it might burst from her chest. "Of course I'll build a life with you at La Vida. I love it there almost as much as I love you. Besides," she shrugged one shoulder, "you need a pastry chef."

A devilish smile lit up his face. "Are you thinking about applying for the job?"

"Sure. As long as you promise to perform an extensive and exhausting interview. You know... just to make sure we're a good fit."

"Honey, we're the perfect fit," he murmured, pulling her into his arms. "I love you, Sage, and I plan to prove it to you every day for the rest of our lives."

She grinned. "Sounds like a great plan."

"You want me to tell you about it?" he asked, his voice low, rough, and sexy as sin.

"Nope." She slipped her arms around his shoulders, stretched to her tiptoes in the sand, and brushed her lips against his. "I want you to show me."

EPILOGUE

SAGE pulled a batch of chocolate croissants from La Vida's oven, closed her eyes, and drew in a deep breath of buttery goodness. *Heavenly.* Exhaling a contented sigh, she carefully placed them on a rack to cool and stepped back to admire her work.

Thrilled to turn in her laptop for an apron, she'd taken over as La Vida's pastry chef the day she'd returned to Costa Rica.

"They smell amazing," Pax murmured, coming up behind her. He wrapped his arms around her waist and pulled her firmly against his chest. "Almost as good as you do," he added in a throaty whisper as he nibbled her neck.

Sage grinned and tipped her head further to the side. "If you're trying to sweet talk me into giving you a croissant, it's kind of working."

"Only kind of?" He nipped her ear, making her best parts perk up in interest.

"I've got to make sure there are enough for the guests before I start exchanging them for sexual favors. I take my new career very seriously." She closed her eyes and moaned in appreciation as his tongue found the sensitive spot directly behind her ear. "Okay, maybe you can have one."

She felt him grin along her neck and knew they either needed to stop or, better yet, find somewhere private to continue.

"How many croissants could I get for—"

The sound of Pax's mobile phone ringing cut his offer short. Reluctantly pulling free from his embrace, Sage opened her eyes and turned to watch him glance at his phone's screen.

He blew out a breath. "It's Mom. She probably wants to talk about Kat again. Apparently she's been distracted since returning to Silver Bay. Mom thinks I know why."

"Do you?"

"Nope. Kat left La Vida by her own choice and seemed happy to do so."

"I'll check on Kat later today. You talk to your mom while I finish up in here. Then we can find somewhere private to pick up where we left off," she said with a wink.

His eyes flashed then darkened. "I'll be quick," he promised and tapped his phone to answer. "Hey, Mom."

Sage watched Pax's expression go from determined to surprised as he listened.

"Yeah, I'm sure he'd be interested," he said a moment later. "Okay, I'll talk to him and get back to you. Bye, Mom. Love you too."

Still looking a little stunned, Pax slipped the phone into his pocket and leaned back against the counter. He opened his mouth. Shut it. Then cocked his head to the side before turning to look at her. "Mom just asked if Logan would be interested in helping add a community outreach program to Bennett Industry's charity foundation. She said what we're doing at La Vida inspired her to make the foundation more hands-on in its approach."

"I'm not surprised. Your parents love it here and are proud of what you've created. Wait." Sage stepped closer and placed her hand on his chest, "Are you upset they asked Logan to help and not you?"

"Not at all," Pax said, his tone emphatic. "Mom said she knew you and I were needed here but hoped La Vida could spare Logan for a few months this summer. She even has a free place for him to stay."

"That's great. Logan will love Silver Bay, and he keeps talking about wanting to visit the States. Sounds like a win-win situation."

"I guess." Pax shook his head. "But it felt like she wasn't telling me the whole story."

"I'm sure that's just part of being a mom." Sage grinned and stepped around Pax to return her apron to the hook. "Holy buckets. Is that Carter O'Reilly?" She stared through the front window in shock as the movie star climbed from the Land Rover.

"Yeah, he's due to arrive today. He visits a couple of times a year. He's pretty good friends with Brick."

"You're kidding," Sage sputtered. "I thought he made that up."

"Nope. Brick is a straight shooter."

"But what about all those other stories? What about skiing off the mountain cliff? Did that really happen?"

"Yep."

"Chasing a bank robber on foot?"

"Uh-huh."

"Even training a race horse for the Kentucky Derby?" She was incredulous. All of his stories were real?

"Brick has lived a full life." Pax nodded matter-of-factly. "Speaking of full lives, you've been working too hard. Time for a break." He scooped her into his arms.

"Where are we going?" she asked on a bubble of laughter as he strode from the kitchen.

"Remember that very private waterfall I showed you before?"

"Yep." She bit her lip in anticipation.

"I thought we could play castaway there for the rest of the day, enjoying some hijinks and adventures."

"Hmm. Sounds really piratey."

"I know how much you like pirates," Pax said, carrying her from the hacienda.

"Do I have to call you captain?" she asked.

He grinned wickedly down at her. "No. But I'll make it worth your while if you do. What do you say? Up for an adventure?"

"Aye, captain," Sage murmured in a husky voice, threading her hands through his dark hair. "With you, I'm always up for an adventure."

Thank You!

Thanks for reading A Venture of the Heart. *I hope you enjoyed it!*

While much of Sage and Pax's adventure took place in Costa Rica, book two in the series is set in the Bennett family's hometown of Silver Bay, Wisconsin and will be released in the spring of 2017. If you'd like an email when it's released, please visit www.ameliajudd.com to sign up for my newsletter.

I've included an excerpt from book two, Crashing Together. *The story features Kat and Logan's romance and was an absolute blast to write! I hope you enjoy these two characters as much as I do...*

Happy reading!
Amelia

CRASHING TOGETHER

A Silver Bay Romance
Coming in Spring of 2017

Kat Bennett needs a place to stay. By tonight. So when her brother's best friend, Logan McCabe, offers up his spare room for the duration of the summer, she accepts even though common sense has always warned her to steer clear of the gorgeous Australian with a boyish smile and a knack for breaking female hearts. Spending time with Logan, however, quickly convinces Kat she needs to change tactics and embrace temptation rather than fight it. After all, a steamy fling would be the perfect distraction from real-life problems, and who better to fling with than a gorgeous commitmentphobe who's only in the country for a few months?

With no ties holding him down, carefree Logan is able to enjoy any of the beautiful places and many of the beautiful women the world has to offer. And he does. Or at least he did right up until the moment he impulsively invites Kat, a woman he has vowed not to touch, to live with him for the summer. Being close to the gorgeous, fiery, and completely off-limits Kat shoots Logan's relaxed vibe to hell and, even worse, makes him begin to question the safe, unattached lifestyle he's vowed to maintain...

ONE

"Come on, baby, just a little bit more."

Kat Bennett's body strained, and her arms shook as she pleaded with the stubborn iron rod in her hands. Who knew lug nuts could be so tight? Getting them off at home would've been a lot easier, but she hadn't noticed anything wrong when she'd left this morning. It took the stomach-dropping, telltale thumping of a flat tire for her to realize the powers that be still enjoyed a good laugh at her expense.

She was stuck, her cell-phone battery drained, along a deserted two-lane road on a blisteringly hot Wisconsin afternoon. The stagnant humid air clung to her skin, sweat dripped down her face, and mosquitos buzzed around her ears. Figured she would get a flat tire on the hottest frickin' day of the summer.

Even though she'd only been stranded for half an hour, the hundred-degree heat index and her wrestling match with the iron-willed lug nuts had sent both her temperature and her temper into the red zone.

Thanks to the step-by-step directions in her owner's manual, she'd managed to locate the spare tire and figured out how to use the jack. It ticked her off that she'd gotten as far as lifting her tire six inches off the ground but couldn't budge the damn lug nuts. And the realization that a big, brawny guy could probably do it in a few seconds *really* ticked her off.

Kat blew the mosquitos from her face, tightened her grip on the smooth tire iron, and braced her feet in the gravel. Redoubling her efforts, she threw every ounce of her one hundred and five pounds into the job. When she failed to budge the damn thing a fraction of an inch, she dropped to her butt and cursed vividly.

Yesterday, her car's air conditioner had died. The day before that, she'd gotten a ticket for going a perfectly reasonable speed—in her opinion—and now this. Couldn't the universe give her one frickin' day without some sort of drama, complication, or issue?

She tensed at the sound of a vehicle approaching from the opposite direction. Sitting between her car and the grassy ditch, she couldn't see the type of car, but the engine's low purr suggested the sort of sports car usually favored by men. Her heart knocked in her chest when she heard its tires crunch over the gravel as it pulled onto the shoulder across the road.

"No, no, no," she mumbled to herself. "Don't stop. Please, don't stop."

This was the first car to even slow down. Not that there'd been many cars. Few took the scenic route to Sheboygan, the nearest "big town" to Silver

Bay. Most drivers opted for the highway a few miles to the west that ran parallel to the narrow, winding road she'd chosen on her trip home from one of the many responsibilities she'd unwittingly accumulated over the past few weeks.

In all fairness, she'd hidden from view the few times other cars had passed by, so the drivers had probably assumed there was no one stranded to help. Logically, she knew anyone who stopped would likely be a friendly Silver Bay resident. But she still felt trapped and vulnerable.

She used to be strong and fearless. Now she cowered.

God, that pissed her off.

She flipped from her butt to her hands and knees. Ignoring the bite of the gravel digging into her skin, she peered under her car. Her mouth went dry and her pulse beat heavy in her throat as a set of male feet stepped from a low-slung red car.

She needed to find a weapon in case the guy wasn't a kind local. Scanning the ground, she spotted the tire iron. She snatched up the heavy rod and stood, holding her impromptu weapon along the length of her leg. No sense swinging for the bleachers if her visitor turned out to be friend rather than foe.

One look at him and the certainty of trouble slammed into her.

He stood well over six feet tall—his broad, muscular physique at least doubling her own weight. His surfer-boy blond hair, deep tan, and the stubble on his sculpted jaw made it clear he didn't spend his time in an office. A smile played around his full mouth as she met his gorgeous blue eyes. He bordered on perfection. And dammit, for some inexplicable reason that pissed her off even more than her weakness had moments ago.

"Heard you were in town." Kat kept her voice flat and her expression bored. No way would she let Logan McCabe realize how much he got to her.

"Arrived a week ago. Been hoping to see you around." His eyes lit with good-natured humor. "Nice to see you again, darl. We miss you at La Vida." His tantalizing Australian accent shot a hot jolt of awareness straight to her good parts.

Seriously? Why could her body never behave around this guy?

Last winter, she'd spent a month at La Vida de Ensueño, an environmentally friendly, socially responsible resort in Costa Rica that her brother, Paxton, owned. At first, Kat hadn't wanted to leave the natural beauty, friendly people, and sense of purpose she'd found at La Vida. But her attraction to Logan, her brother's best friend and the resort's reigning Casanova, had eventually convinced her otherwise.

Too big, too flirty, too tempting, too much trouble. Within moments of meeting him, Kat had summed him up with those four too's. She'd tried her damnedest to ignore him. Which worked about as well as trying to ignore a tornado hovering at the edge of her peripheral vision. Even when she managed to not look at him, she always knew he was there and could turn her world upside down without even noticing.

"It's nice to hear I've been missed," she said, "but I can't imagine Pax and Sage coming up for air long enough to notice I'm gone."

Logan grinned. "True. Those two are in their own little world. The rest of us miss you though. You lived there for five or six months before leaving, ay?"

"One," she snarled, shoving back dark strands of hair that had escaped from her ponytail. *Un-frickin'-believable.* He'd haunted every day of her stay at La Vida, and the jerkface didn't even have a clue how long she'd spent there.

"Huh." He shrugged. "Seemed longer."

She did a mental eye roll, then took in the low-riding black boardshorts and the stretchy blue swim shirt clinging so tightly that his chest resembled a detailed topographic map. His body had more hills, bluffs, and ridges than the Driftless Area National Wildlife Refuge.

Too damn hot. Adding another "too" to her list, she resisted fanning herself with her own hand.

"Going surfing?" While his outfit made it obvious he was headed for a swim, the board strapped to the roof explained why he was on the road to Sheboygan.

"Yip. Heard the funny sounding town south of here is the 'Malibu of the Midwest.' Had to give it a go." His gaze dropped to her flat tire. "Need a hand?"

"Nope. Almost done here."

He shifted his baby blues from the flat tire still attached to her car and studied her with a look of skeptical intrigue. "Lug nuts stuck?"

"No." Okay, maybe she'd snapped the reply a little too quickly in retrospect. But how the hell had he figured that out?

"Time for you to leave." She motioned for him

to go with a few backward flicks of her fingers. "Buh-bye."

"Sorry, can't leave until you do." He gestured to the tire iron she was white-knuckling in her right hand. "Now are you going take a swing at me with that thing or use it to get your tire off?"

She glared for a long moment. "Not sure. Maybe both."

"Fair enough. Let me know when you decide." Logan began whistling a happy little tune and rocked back on his heels, looking around the tree-lined road with an expression of casual interest.

The bastard.

Kat grunted, spun on her heel, and shoved the end of the two-foot rod onto one of the stubborn lug nuts with a little more force than necessary. No way would she let him change the damn tire. She *so* did not need his help. She gripped the rod, scrunched her eyes closed, and started to compose a little mental prayer to Hercules.

"One time," Logan said, interrupting her plea to the Greek hero, "I watched my mum change a tire when I was an ankle-biter. She angled the tire iron so that it came off the nut at about eleven o'clock, assuming the lug nut is the center of a clock. Then she turned around and stepped onto the rod with all her weight. It was an ace move."

Damn. That might actually work.

Without looking back, Kat adjusted the wrench to the correct angle, straightened, took a deep breath, and stepped up and onto the lever with her right foot. In one smooth motion, the lever gently lowered to the ground. *Yes!* Flying high from success, she quickly loosened the other nuts, removed the flat tire, and slipped on the new one. Minutes later, she'd tightened the spare tire into place and lowered her car back to the ground.

While Logan watched the whole process, he never tried to take over. She had to give him credit. Her petite size usually made guys try to do everything for her. Which, of course, ticked her off.

She put the last tool into the trunk and slammed it shut in triumph. With a quick bubble of laughter, she turned to Logan. "I did it!" Her smile dropped at his look of sharp interest. "What?" she demanded.

"First time you've ever really smiled at me," he said, his accent thicker than usual.

Locked in his intense gaze, she remained motionless, unsure if she wanted to remember, ruin, or ignore the moment.

A few heavy breaths later, he grinned and shook his head as if breaking from a trance. "Blinded me for a minute."

His words sent an unwanted wave of warmth and desire through her. *Ugh.* She had to put an end to the weird connection that started building between them at La Vida. Time to slip back into her edgy 'tude.

"You're full of shit, Logan. Now get the hell out of here before I change my mind and start beating you with that tire iron after all."

He laughed and lifted is hands in a palms-out, no-harm-meant gesture. "I'm sensing some hostility."

She crossed her arms and cocked an eyebrow. "What tipped you off?"

"The repeated threats of violence mostly." He tilted his head and studied her. "What is it about me that gets you so worked up, darl?"

Fighting back the growl building in her throat, Kat drew in a breath and narrowed her eyes. "Well, I won't use the phrase 'manwhore' because—"

"Think you just did," he interrupted.

"Because," she repeated more firmly, "I'm sure there's never been an exchange of money. But I can't respect a guy who changes women more often than I change shoes."

"It's not like I sleep with a different woman every night."

"Maybe. But you don't stick. When's the last time you dated anyone longer than a month?"

"Long-term isn't my specialty." Logan shrugged. "I'm sure you can relate."

"Relate? How?" Kat demanded. "I don't bounce from one bed to the next."

"Sure of that? In the last year you've moved from DC to Silver Bay to Costa Rica where you stayed with Sage, then Pax, then Susanna before moving back to Silver Bay again. That's a lot more beds than I've slept in."

"I slept in those beds alone," she said between clenched teeth. "You didn't."

"And that upsets you?"

"Of course not," she snapped. "I couldn't care less who you sleep with."

"Doesn't this entire conversation prove otherwise?"

Kat threw her arms in the air. "God, you're exhausting!"

Logan flashed a boyish smile. "Thanks."

She growled in frustration and pointed down the road. "We're done here. Thanks for stopping. Now leave."

He dipped his head in mock concession. "Alright, alright. I'll go." He crossed back to his car and opened the driver's door. "You're heading home, right?"

"Yep. Straight home. No problem. Got it covered. Buh-bye."

He climbed into his car. "I'll follow you to make sure that spare tire holds." He slammed the door shut before she could respond.

No frickin' way. She did not need him hovering over her like some paranoid helicopter parent on the playground.

"No thanks," she yelled over the sound of his car's engine purring to life. "Don't follow me. Just go surfing." She gestured dramatically in the direction of Sheboygan with both hands like an overenthusiastic ground's crewman at the airport.

Logan revved the engine. "Can't hear you," he mouthed through the window, cupping a hand behind his ear. He added a wolfish smile capable of melting the panties off any mortal woman.

"Fine. Whatever," she muttered, throwing her hands up in frustration. Logan always did whatever the hell he wanted anyway.

She stormed into her driver's seat. It totally pissed her off that he was right about how his behavior could get her "so worked up." Her last week in Costa Rica served as an excellent case in point. When a group of youngish women checked into La Vida itching to celebrate some sort of minor career accomplishment, Logan had taken it upon himself to make sure they had the frickin' time of their lives. Kat had spent a teeth-grinding week watching him hit on anything with two legs and a pair of breasts. She'd managed to keep her irritation to herself—for the most part at least—until the night she saw him walking toward one of the villas with a drunk woman on each arm and an infuriating grin on his face.

That's when she'd lost it. The details were thankfully a little fuzzy—blinding rage could apparently do that to a person—but Kat did remember storming to her villa, throwing her stuff into a suitcase, and booking a ticket back to Silver Bay. Sure, she had no claim on Logan, but she'd been instantly attracted to him in Costa Rica. Watching the asshole take two women to bed was more than she could stand.

Kat continued her mental rant about him for most of the drive home. At least her irritation with Logan kept her from thinking about the "talk" her parents wanted to have with her. She had a pretty good idea what the "talk" would be about, and she wasn't looking forward to another grilling. Not that she had much of a choice. Except for the month at La Vida last winter, she'd been living with them at her childhood home since moving back from Washington DC almost a year ago.

Tonight would be another one of the heart-to-hearts her folks insisted on having every few months. *Why did you quit your job? Why did you leave DC? What are you going to do with your life now? Why keep floating from job to job? Why have you been even more distracted since leaving Costa Rica?* Blah. Blah. Blah.

No way in hell she'd tell anyone the real reason she'd quit her job and moved home to Silver Bay, least of all her overprotective parents.

Kat turned down the tree-lined drive to their estate and parked her car in one of the extra spaces beside the four-car garage on the left side of the sprawling lakefront house. She tipped her head from side to side and enjoyed the rewarding cracking of her neck. Then she blew out a breath and plastered on a smile.

Time to put on her game face.

She hopped out of her car, hoping to make it inside before Logan arrived. At least he hadn't been tailing her that closely, but she knew he'd show up sooner or later. Even though he had his share of flaws, Logan genuinely liked to help people. Hopefully, once he saw her car parked by the garage he'd continue around the circular drive and head right back out on the road and away from her.

She hustled to the side door. The thick humid air clung to her and added another layer of yuck to her already filthy skin. She glanced at her phone and groaned. Her little tire-changing adventure had eaten into the time she'd allotted for showering before dinner. Guess hot-and-sweaty would be her look for this family meeting.

The moment she stepped into the mudroom her parents' three-year-old golden retriever, Cosmo, bounded toward her with one of his many stuffed animals gripped in his mouth.

"Hey, buddy. Did you miss me today?" Kat kneeled to pet his head and received multiple licks to the face.

Cosmo's whole body wagged with excitement. Every time she walked through the door, his jubilant, better-than-Christmas-morning reaction made her feel like a superstar. Sure would be nice if everyone greeted her with that kind of enthusiasm.

Kat dropped a quick kiss on his smooth head. "Sorry, boy. I have to clean up. I promise to give you some extra belly rubs later."

She moved into the half bath attached to the mudroom, washed the grease from her hands, splashed cold water on her face, and redid her ponytail. "Good as it's going to get," she said into the mirror.

A moment before she rounded the corner into the kitchen, she heard her parents enter the room from the other side.

"She's going to be furious," her mom said.

"I'm aware of that, but she can't live here any longer," her dad replied, conviction filling his voice. "She walked away from a promising career in international affairs for no apparent reason. She's twenty-eight years old, doesn't have a job, and lives with her parents."

Her mom sighed. "Maybe she needs a little more time."

"It has been almost a year since she left DC and almost five months since she got back from Costa Rica. I am happy to help our children when they are trying to make something of themselves, but Katherine isn't even trying. We cannot enable this behavior any longer. It's time for her to move forward with her life." Her dad's voice shook with frustration. "I don't understand when she got so damn lazy!"

Kat's gut clenched, and her heart pounded. Shame washed through her, flooding her eyes with tears. God, she wanted her old life back. She wanted to feel strong again even if it had only been a false sense of strength. Ignorance truly was bliss. One mistake had taught her the truth. She was weak. And even if she hid her cowardice from everyone else, that truth would always haunt her.

Pushing back the hurt, she tipped her chin up, and stepped into the kitchen doorway before she had to hear any more about the loser she'd become. "No worries," she said in a neutral voice. "I'm happy to find somewhere else to live."

Her parents flinched and turned to look at her.

"Kat, honey. We didn't know you were there." Her mom took a step forward, her face tight with concern.

Kat extended her hand to stop her. "It's fine. Dad's right. I am too old to live at home. Probably best if I look for somewhere else to stay tonight."

She turned and stumbled out of the house, desperate to leave before they saw the tears threatening to spill down her cheeks. She'd meant what she'd said—she was too old to live with her parents.

Problem was, she was too damn afraid to live alone.

Crashing Together *is now available for preorder. If you'd like to receive an email when I release a new book, please visit www.ameliajudd.com to sign up for my newsletter.*

About the Author

Award-winning author Amelia Judd writes fun and flirty contemporary romance. She loves to entertain her readers with memorable characters and fast-paced plots that blend humor, heart, and heat.

After receiving a degree in international affairs, Amelia lived and studied in Belgium for over three years. During her time in Europe, she traveled extensively, earned a master's degree, and fell in love with writing contemporary romance.

Amelia now lives in the Midwest with her sports-loving husband, two active kids, and a lovable dog that insists on staying by her side day and night. When she isn't writing, she's spending time with family, hanging out with friends, chauffeuring her kiddos around town, or planning her family's next getaway.

Connect with Amelia Judd online:

www.ameliajudd.com

www.facebook.com/author.amelia.judd/

amelia@ameliajudd.com